Other Books by T.K. Galarneau

A Cowboy Tradition: Poems From the Heart
Meadow Muffins in the Trail
Ruminations of an Old Woman

The
Arrangement

THE
Arrangement

T.K. Galarneau

Dusty Rose Books
Bedazzled Ink Publishing Company • Fairfield, California

paperback 978-1-949290-70-7

Cover Design
by

Dusty Rose Books
a division of
Bedazzled Ink Publishing, LLC
Fairfield, California
http://www.bedazzledink.com

To Marilynn Uhart, my favorite cousin . . .

Harmony

A way of life that's so sublime
O'er blown with sands of time.

A harmony so at peace
With nature's bounty never ceased.

A love above all others shone
Like a light from heaven alone.

Only grew with kind, loving care
The Creator left room to spare.

So that all on earth could see
Their mother's face would truly be

A beacon through many outrageous storms
Would keep us safe when nature performs

Her frightening dance to cleanse the world
Of all the damage from human's hurled

At their home from ignorance and greed
Replacing common sense for what we need.

Mother Earth the Creator's masterpiece
Is not our own, but is merely a lease.

How can we destroy what we don't own
A home that's meant for those unborn.

When will we learn when we devastate
The earth where we live our only fate

On this planet like a desert so desolate
Is to die with our mother we desecrate.

Let us all pray that soon we return
To life as intended and that we spurn

This headlong crash that won't set us free
Only an honorable life leads to harmony.

Reflection

As time moves on year upon year
We're faced with a fact so clear.

Our time on Mother Earth grows short
We're left to question our place of course.

In the overall scheme of the universe
And all the Great Spirit's biodiverse

Creations meant to live in peace
For millenniums without surcease.

Our obligations are sure and clear
To leave the earth clean and pure

For future generations to come
Without fear that we might succumb

To living only for this day alone
And leave the earth a combat zone

Bereft of life and just a cornerstone
Of what was once a paradise sown

With all flora and fauna man might need
To live for all eternity provided he heed

A warning from Creator and not abuse
The living things that man could choose

To help him survive but leave for children
Of future generations those kindred

Spirits, like minded souls who save the earth
And all there upon live in harmony and mirth.

Reverence for the Land

Papa asked me out of hand,
"When you look at the land,
Please tell me what you see?
Do we pay or own it for free?"

"Tell me true, but think it through.
Don't answer me 'til you're sure."
I scanned the ground and hills afar
I knew for sure I weren't no superstar

At figuring my pa's peculiar puzzle
I'd as soon as not get in a tussle,
With an ailing yearling heifer
That ate a load of 'buffalo burr'.

I'd used 'bout all the time I had
For pa would think I was bad
At figurin' his simple little quiz
Since we was in the land usin' biz.

"Pa I see what the Creator gave
He could take away with a wave
If we don't try with all our might
To use His property just right."

I said my piece and stayed stalk still.
I hoped my answer would fit the bill
Or I'd get a lecture 'bout responsibility.
I had some of them to test my civility.

"That's all ya want to say?" Papa asked of me.
A little voice was proddin' to best not let this be
The end of my answer and might I not agree
With pa there was still much more I could see.

"Well pa," I replied. "There's more than just land
Of course. There's livestock that carry our brand.
We raise our cows and hay in hopes that we can live.
On the earth with all the bounty that she gives.

"Most of all I think I see the earth as our loving mother
To whom we show respect and love above all the others.

The Arrangement

SHELLS EXPLODED ALL around Quinn's position on the hill. He had been pinned down for the better part of three days. The rebel army had overrun the union's position and his cavalry regiment had been cut to pieces by the confederate artillery. To say Quinn's situation was dire was an obvious understatement. Every time Quinn tried to move, either a shell or sniper made redeployment impossible. Probably the worst part of being pinned down was not being able to help his comrades. The cries of dying men were impossible to ignore. In addition, the hot summer days only aided in the rapid decay of the dead. The putrefying flesh of both humans and horses created a stench from which Quinn could not escape.

The Battle of Gettysburg, July 1 to 3, 1863, all but ended General Robert E. Lee's invasion of the north. The estimates of total casualties [on both sides] were over 57,000. The battle also ended Quinn's military career. After he walked away, he returned to his father's farm in Ohio only to find his two older brothers were killed six months prior at Chancellorsville in May. His younger brother Flynn had headed west in '61 to try his hand as a buckaroo. The war had taken a huge toll on the Duncan family, but Quinn seemed to suffer most . . . even more so than his dead brothers. For them, the war was truly over; for Quinn, he would continue to fight the war for the next twenty-five years.

"Son," Colin Duncan inquired, "will you resume your practice now the war—for you—is over?"

Quinn could barely string a whole sentence together let alone an entire conversation. He rarely spoke to anyone, he kept to himself, and spent most of his time with the horses. The thought of reopening his medical practice was as foreign to him as sleeping through the night without reliving a bloody battle. He was a broken man.

"No, pa," Quinn replied. "How can these hands regain the soft touch required of a healer? These hands that bashed the skulls of my fellow man to bloody pulps. Hands that have blown men to pieces. Hands that have choked the life from another human being. Nope, not me."

"My boy," Colin said softly. "You aren't the only man who has killed in this bloody struggle. You did what was required of a soldier. You did what was expected of you; you cannot continue to punish yourself for that."

"Pa," Quinn said morosely. "I took an oath in medical school to save lives, to do no harm. I could have stayed in a field hospital, but I didn't. I volunteered to take life."

"What will you do then?" the older Duncan asked.

"I'm going west," Quinn replied.

THE COLORADO ROCKIES seemed to stretch on forever and were the most imposing mountain range in the western United States. They were as brutal as they were imposing; they had taken countless lives of those who underestimated their brutality. Still, as imposing as they were, there was a certain peacefulness and isolation. The isolation was what most appealed to Quinn. Upon leaving his father's farm, Quinn booked passage on a paddle wheeler down the Ohio River to the Missouri. At Independence, he bought horses, mules, and the supplies he would need with which to prospect. He wasn't concerned as much with finding gold as he was just getting away from people . . . and truth be told from himself. He wasn't concerned with the wisdom of this journey. As a matter of fact, if he died in this endeavor that would be fine as well. However, he was to find out that his will to live was much stronger than his wish to die.

Two years had passed since Gettysburg; the war had finally ended. The period of reconstruction would be almost as deadly as the war. A president had been assassinated, carpetbaggers invaded the south lookin' to get rich on the misfortune of others, and a body of thugs, primarily enraged southerners, organized the KKK. Fortunately, high in the Rockies, Quinn was sheltered from all that. The war hadn't completely destroyed his humanity; however, the mountains certainly hardened him. He learned to live off the land; he gained an affinity with nature; he had learned to live like the Arapaho and Cheyenne who lived in this country. He became known to them as White Bear: Nonoocoo Woxuum [Arapaho] and Vo`kohe Nan`kohe [Cheyenne]. The name certainly applied: Quinn was a huge man and like a bear pretty much kept to himself. So the Indians pretty much left him to his own devices. On the few occasions he interacted with the Indians, he did so to get fresh horses. The Cheyenne traded with the Nez Perce who bred colored horses, Appaloosas, and he traded his mules for three nice ponies. He had no idea why the Cheyenne were interested in Quinn's mules. But both parties got what they wanted and no one was harmed. Hardly the political line the government was espousing: "the only good Indian was a dead Indian."

Quinn spent the better part of three years roaming around the mountains searching for gold, but mostly just living off the land. The mountains were a refuge for Quinn. He had time to think and forget. The war ended in 1865 and in 1868, the government had a new pastime: taking land from the various tribes who lived in the west. Westward expansion was running full tilt. The construction of the transcontinental railroad was well underway and the discovery of gold on Indian lands would bring the inevitable destruction of Native American people and their way of life. With this backdrop, Quinn came down out of the mountains on a journey of redemption, a return to the world of men, with all their foibles.

NEW MEXICO TERRITORY in 1868 was a land in transition, from land belonging to the native tribes to land belonging to farmers and ranchers. Needless to say, land ownership did not change hands without conflict. Jicarilla Apache inhabited the land. Of all the Native tribes, the Apache were the fiercest fighters and most feared by Natives and whites alike. The last thing Quinn wanted was trouble with Indians or whites. He kept a sharp lookout for anything amiss and just rode on. He finally reached the end of his journey the first part of June, 1868 . . . a small town called La Cueva in the foothills of the Sangre de Cristo Mountains. He hoped he'd be welcomed, but if not, he'd simply ride on.

"One thing I never expected to see was a cow puncher behind a mule and a plow." Quinn laughed.

A man nearly as big as Quinn hollered and his mule stopped; he turned to face Quinn. The man had a deep gravelly voice.

"At least my digging in the dirt will result in food for my family and stock," the man replied tersely. "What will a man diggin' in hard rock, in a futile attempt to find gold, ever accomplish?"

Quinn dug in his saddle bags and tossed the man two bags filled with twenty dollar gold pieces.

"What'd ya do?" The man laughed. "Give up prospectin' and start robbin' banks?"

"No," Quinn stated. "I found enough gold for my needs, then sold the claim and let some other damn fool dig in the rocks. I headed south."

A woman in her late thirties came around the house followed by a boy of fifteen and a girl about seven or eight. She was an attractive woman, but the years of working the land were starting to show. Hopefully Quinn's contribution would make life a little easier on this family. Quinn had found his brother, Flynn, and to his surprise, he had a family.

"Well," Flynn growled, "ya better get down and give that poor horse some rest."

Quinn dismounted and the two brothers embraced and clapped each other on the back. The embrace was a jovial affair between two men who hadn't seen each other for seven years.

"Gwenny, I want you to meet my brother, Quinn. Quinn my wife and kids: Hank and Katie."

Not wanting to seem too familiar, Quinn extended his hand to Gwenny, but she would have none of that. She stepped forward and pulled Quinn to her in a friendly, welcoming embrace. Hank reached out his hand to shake Quinn's. Katie was a little more reserved, but Quinn found the sense to kneel down and kindly, gently say hello.

"Hello, Katie," Quinn said softly. "I'm very glad to meet you."

For her part, Katie must have sensed Quinn's inner pain; the same pain she felt at the loss of her father. She felt safe enough to walk forward and fall into Quinn's protective embrace. When she spoke, she spoke from her heart.

"I'm glad to meet you too," she replied in a soft, shy voice.

There was an awkward silence between the two until Flynn spoke up.

"Well I imagine you'd like to clean up and rest from your long ride. There's a mineral spring up the hill behind the house. You can have a good hot soak. That'd be good for your old bones."

Quinn raised an eyebrow and looked disdainfully at his brother.

"What do you me old?" Quinn remarked. "I'm not that much older than you and at least my hair isn't grey."

Still, truth be told, Quinn was glad of his good fortune and would surely love a good soak.

"Let me tend to my horses and I'll take you up on the offer."

"I'll take care of your horses, sir," Hank said cheerfully.

"Thank you son," Quinn replied, "and my name is Quinn not sir."

"Alright . . . Quinn," Hank said as he led Quinn's horses to the corral.

With his saddlebags slung over his shoulder, Quinn walked the short distance to the spring. He eased his aching body down into the hot water. The mineral water had the instant effect of untying the knots in his muscles and relieving his aching head. After his soak, Quinn met Hank as he rounded the corner of the house.

"I grained your horses and brought your rifle and bedroll into the house, sir, I mean Quinn."

"Thank you, Hank, I appreciate that. Those horses haven't had grain in quite a spell. They're used to prairie grass. Shoot, grain must be like candy to them."

Gwenny outdid herself for dinner. She fixed a bison roast, potatoes and gravy, fresh carrots, and biscuits with wild honey. This was the first home cooked meal Quinn had in years.

"Gwenny this was sure a fine meal. Thank you," Quinn remarked.

"You're most welcome, Quinn. I thought we'd have a celebratory meal to welcome you," Gwenny replied. "Actually, cooking over the hearth isn't too difficult. Everything can be cooked in one big pot. I bake the biscuits in a Dutch oven on the coals."

"Well, however you made this meal, I don't remember having anything finer." Then Quinn added, "Flynn, you're one lucky fella."

"Yes I am," Flynn said. "Yes indeed."

"If you two don't stop, all these compliments might go to my head." Gwenny laughed. "Why don't you men make yourselves scarce so Hank, Katie, and I can clean up the dishes?"

"C'mon, Quinn," Flynn said. "Let's go out and have a smoke. We can talk awhile."

The New Mexico evening air was cool and clean this time of year. Later in July that was another thing. The two men sat in the front yard enjoying one another's company. Flynn related how he and Gwenny met, fell in love, and got married. Her first husband was killed when a stray bullet passed through the wall of a saloon and hit him. He happened to be in the wrong place at the wrong time. He had gone into La Cueva, near Fort Union, to buy cattle. The small town had sprung up after the town's founder, Vincente Romero, figured being close to the fort would be safer in case of Apache attacks.

Since the ranch was some distance from town, and they received few visitors, Gwenny and the children lived alone for some time before news of Jeremy's death reached them. As a result of his death, they had a pretty tough time for the better part of a year. Close to June 1866, Flynn came stumbling onto Gwenny's place with a bullet lodged in his back. He and another puncher had been trailing a hundred head of steers to La Cueva to sell. About halfway there, rustlers attacked them, killed his companion, shot Flynn, and made off with the cattle. Fortunately for Flynn, Gwenny brought him back to health, which took a while. Flynn was determined to go after the men who "done him wrong." Since he was as stubborn as the orneriest of any mule, no amount of convincing, on Gwenny's part, would do any good. Flynn took off after the rustlers; he found them in La Cueva getting drunk at the local watering hole. There was a gun battle, the rustlers were killed, and luckily, Flynn recovered his stolen cattle. Flynn intended to travel up north, but he was smitten with the widow and her children. He decided the time had come for him to settle down, so he returned to Gwenny's ranch. They'd been together for two years by the time Quinn showed up.

"So, that's how I became a respectable rancher." Flynn laughed. "We still have a lot to do to fix up this place and make it pay. First off, every dime we get will go into the house and make it more livable for Gwenny and the kids. She deserves better than a dirt floor."

"Well, then," Quinn remarked, "I expect we oughta do something about that."

"I don't recollect any money trees growin' 'round here," Flynn surmised.

"Listen," Quinn responded, "if I'm gonna hang around here for a spell, I plan to contribute to the cause. I ain't gonna be free loadin'. 'Sides, I'd just fritter that money away anyway. And when I do come back, I want to feel welcomed."

"You're my brother, Quinn," Flynn whispered. "You don't have to pay to live here."

"Don't matter, little brother." Quinn chuckled. "This is just how things are gonna be."

"Well, I do want to provide a better place for Gwenny and the kids . . ."

"Good." Quinn laughed. "I'm glad that's settled. I was afraid we were gonna come to blows over this."

"Now, let me ask you where you got them spotted ponies?" Flynn inquired.

"I traded for 'em from the Northern Cheyenne in Colorado," Quinn explained. "Traded two saddle horses and three mules. Don't have any idea what they wanted them mules for, but they got 'em. I figure I might get me a piece of land somewhere and raise Appaloosas."

"Don't think I haven't noticed you haven't mentioned anything about ma and pa . . . or the war," Flynn stated.

"The folks are fine," Quinn replied. "Pa's still workin' the farm. He's got help so he doesn't have to do the heavy work. Ma's the same . . . worries too much about pa . . . and you. Wonders if she'll ever see you again. And the war is best left to the dead and be done with."

"You talked about raising cattle, horses, and prospectin', but nothin' about practicin' medicine again," Flynn wondered. "Why?"

A long, awkward silence followed Flynn's question. After some reflection, Flynn was sorry he brought up the subject.

"Look, Quinn." Flynn sighed. "I'm sorry if I hit a sore spot; I was just wonderin'."

"Brother," Quinn replied, "I think we'd better have a family discussion. The time has come for truth . . . no more hiding. You all have the right to know . . . as long as I'm staying here. C'mon."

Both men went into the house; Flynn called for the children to come inside. Quinn facing the fireplace, Flynn's family gathered around facing Quinn. This conversation would be difficult, but might be cathartic as well.

"You all have been very obliging and sociable taking me in and making me feel like I was part of the family," Quinn began.

Flynn interrupted. "You are part of the family . . ."

Quinn raised his hand.

"Please, Flynn," Quinn murmured. "Let me finish without interruption. I'll try to explain things so you'll understand. Although, I'm not sure I fully comprehend everything that's happened in the last five years or so."

"Sorry, brother," Flynn apologized, "go ahead."

"Conner and Ragan left the farm to join the Union Army in the spring of '62. I left in early June. That left ma and pa alone on the farm . . . the war took three of their four sons and the other was gone punchin' cows. I spent two and a half years in that slaughter. I survived Gettysburg, but there were more battles, more killing. I could take no more, so I walked away. I mounted up on a dead man's horse six months before Appomattox. I went home for a bit, but there were too many questions I couldn't answer. I couldn't look into the folks' eyes and make them understand how two of their sons were dead and the one who survived was broken."

Katie watched and listened intently to the big man standing before her. Somehow she knew Quinn was in pain; somehow she understood his need. She got up, sat next to Quinn, and extended her hand. Quinn sat down also, took the small child's hand in his, and continued his story.

"I knew doctors would be at a premium," Quinn continued, "so I signed up to work in any military unit."

Quinn struggled to continue. Obviously, the memories were fresh and raw.

"What I found was the hospital was more like old man Harmon's butcher shop than a hospital," Quinn said. "The sheer size and severity of the wounded was incomprehensible. Most of the doctors were country sawbones and their practices consisted of delivering babies and setting broken bones. They weren't prepared for bodies torn apart by artillery shells and minie balls. Because of the type of injuries that resulted, surgeons more often than not simply amputated limbs to keep soldiers alive. This procedure often failed because soldiers died from gangrene and septicemia. I couldn't be a part of that kind of medicine. But I had volunteered and I couldn't unvolunteer so I joined the first horse outfit I could find. Finally, after Gettysburg and a few more battles, I could take no more, so I commandeered a horse and rode away. I went home to the farm for a while and that was no good either. Ma and Pa expected me to become a farmer since I wasn't going to practice medicine anymore; I wasn't cut out to be a farmer. After two months or so, I headed for Colorado and the gold fields. I figured, if the mountains or Indians didn't kill me, I'd at least get away from people. But what I realized after the first year was that I was trying to get away from myself. After nearly three years, I accomplished two things: I reconciled myself to the events of the war . . . I couldn't let that control me any longer . . . and I made enough money for my lifetime. I sold the claim and came looking for you."

Gwenny and the children were silent throughout the entirety of Quinn's story, but Katie, surprisingly, was the first to speak.

"Uncle Quinn," she began, "I want you to stay here with us forever. I never had an uncle before and I'm glad you are mine."

The small child, with the small voice, spoke the loudest. Hank found his voice too.

"Yes, Uncle Quinn," he agreed. "I want you to stay too."

Gwenny made the final declaration.

"Quinn, the war is over and what happened then can't be undone, so try to put that behind you and be part of our family."

Flynn put the final stamp on the family discussion.

"Welcome home, brother."

"Well, if you are all sure," Quinn replied, "thank you all. I'm proud and happy to be part of the family. And since that's settled, I think tomorrow, Flynn, you should hitch up the wagon, take the family, and head to town for supplies to build onto the house, put a real floor in, and shingle the roof. Take the whole family; I'll stay here and look after things."

The children's eyes lit up like Christmas morning had arrived and old St. Nick left a pile of presents.

"Can we really, ma?" Hank and Katie shouted in unison.

"Yes," Gwenny smiled, "we can all go."

"Quinn," Flynn remarked, "you know this trip will take a couple days. You sure you'll be okay?"

"Really?" Quinn scoffed. "Given that I survived a whole lot in the last few years, I'm sure I can survive for two or three days here by myself. You all take your time; relax a little in town; y'all have earned a little time off."

THE PEACE AND quiet appealed to Quinn. Here on the prairie, with the open space, he was able to sit in front of the house and watch the antelope graze with the cattle. There was plenty of grass to feed the livestock so they didn't stray far. He kept the horses in at night and hobbled his saddle pony during the day and let them all graze. If the horses strayed too far afield, he wouldn't be afoot.

Still, there was plenty to keep him busy. He and Flynn talked about digging a root cellar in the hillside behind the house. They could store extra food to keep them in garden vegetables through the winter. And this winter when the stream iced over, they could cut blocks of ice to put in the root cellar to really keep things cold. They'd be able to butcher a steer and keep the meat cold enough so as not to spoil. Quinn figured that would be a project to get done before the family returned from town. Besides, Quinn was used to wielding a pickaxe and shovel during his prospecting days; he knew he'd have this project done in no time. Quinn had been working for the better part of the morning when (his dog) Rufus began growling. He named Rufus after a black soldier who saved his life during the war. The two men had become good friends, but unfortunately, in order to save Quinn, Rufus forfeited his own life.

"I know, Rufus, quiet boy, I heard 'em," Quinn whispered. "For Apaches, they aren't very quiet. There over there in that stand of junipers. We'll just keep workin' 'til they make their play."

The half dozen Apaches continued to watch the house, corral, and Quinn for another hour or so before they rode up with rifles in plain sight. During the war, Quinn fought off more soldiers at once (single handedly) as well as Northern Cheyenne up in Colorado. Six Apache didn't scare him at all. This wasn't bravado; he knew Apaches were deadly. He didn't consider himself a hero. That's just the way things worked out; hell he was just trying to stay alive.

In broken English, the leader of the group let their intentions be known.

"Spotted ponies. You own?" the man asked.

"Yes," Quinn replied, "they're mine."

"You want sell?" the Apache asked.

"No," Quinn stated. "My horses suit me."

"We kill you and take horses," the Indian declared.

"You can try," Quinn said menacingly. "I'll kill most of you before you kill me."

The Apache leader looked the big man over carefully. Quinn was armed with a Colt revolver, a Winchester rifle, and a Bowie knife which the man was sure Quinn was adept at using. He was thinking he might have broken off more than he could chew. Still he had to save face before his followers. Quinn helped him out.

"Listen," Quinn pronounced. "We don't need to go to war. Get down, we'll smoke a pipe, and parlay."

The Apache grunted.

"Maybe fear Apache?"

"Could be that Apache are afraid of me." Quinn smiled.

This "Mexican standoff" could go one of two ways: the Apache could get down and parlay or there could be a gun battle.

Whatever the case, the Apache warrior lowered his gun and dismounted. The other braves followed suit.

Quinn pointed toward the corral where there was a tree and shade.

"We can sit in the shade and have our smoke."

Quinn went into the house and, to the Apaches' surprise, returned with a pipe and tobacco that was given to him by a Cheyenne chief. Quinn lit the pipe and took a long draw then passed to the Apache leader. Each in turn took a draw on the pipe before the business of parlaying began. The Apache still wanted Quinn's horses, but after three more failed attempts at a trade, he begrudgingly gave up. Still, the trading went on for some time. Quinn presented the Apache leader with a Sharps 50 caliber carbine, a set of leather reins and hackamore, and a couple of fancy knives with elk horn handles. For their part, the Indians gave Quinn a turquoise necklace, two woven saddle blankets, and medicinal herbs to ward off sickness. Finally, when the parlay was at an end, they smoked the pipe once more. In a final friendly gesture, Quinn led the men to the cattle herd and instructed them to cut out two steers to help feed the Apache village through the winter.

The leader of the group finally introduced himself.

"I am called Itzu-Chu, Great Hawk,'" he announced. "This is Jlin Litzoque, Yellow Horse my brother. And Biminah, Slick Roper, Kuruk, Bear, Eskaminzim, Big Mouth. Last is Goyathlay, Yawner. How you called big man?"

"My Cheyenne brothers call me Vo`kohe Nan`kohe, White Bear," Quinn said.

The color drained out of Itzu-Chu's face. Evidently, Quinn's reputation had traveled south.

"Apache know your name. You great white warrior," the man said. "You also healer."

"I was once a warrior and a healer," Quinn remarked, "but no more. I look to raise cattle and horses, but no longer fight wars. Too many people have been killed already. I look to live in peace, but if I have to I will fight to protect my family, just like my Apache brothers."

"We have smoked the pipe," Itzu-Chu said, "There will be peace between us."

The Apache extended his hand which Quinn took in his.

"Yes," Quinn replied, "there will be peace between you and me and my family."

"We are done," the warrior said, "you live here in peace."

FLYNN AND THE family were entertained by Quinn's story of his encounter with the Jicarilla Apaches. Generally, any meet up with Apaches didn't end well, let alone with a peace treaty of sorts.

"You're sure as hell lucky, big brother." Flynn laughed. "How you've lived as long as you have is beyond me."

"Somebody up there must be prayin' for me." Quinn grinned. "Hell, there isn't much danger dealing with the Apache or any Indian really. Just treat them fairly, don't lie to them, and treat them like human beings. Not much to that. They wanted my horses . . . I gave them two of your steers instead."

"Hmmp, that was very generous of you," Flynn grumbled.

"Better than having the whole herd stolen, along with the horses, and me scalped, dontcha think?" Quinn responded.

"Well, I certainly do!" Gwenny exclaimed.

"Me too," the youngsters cried.

"I think you're awfully brave, Uncle Quinn," Katie added.

In order to change the subject of his supposed bravery or luck, Quinn drew everyone's attention to the loaded down wagon.

"Dang, Flynn!" Quinn shouted. "What'd ya do? Buy out the whole general store? You have enough materials here to build two houses and a barn!"

"I don't know about two houses, but there's enough lumber and shingles to fix the house, build a barn, and a bunk house."

"Don't ya think a bunkhouse is a might premature? The outfit isn't quite big enough to hire help," Quinn observed.

Flynn climbed up into the wagon seat and retrieved a bottle of whiskey.

"Alright brother," Flynn said, holding the bottle out to Quinn. "Let's go sit down over yonder and I'll tell you what I have in mind. By the way, this here is good store-bought Scotch whiskey. Better than Pa ever made."

Reluctantly, Quinn walked over to the shade tree and sat down.

"Start explainin', brother."

Quinn took a long swig from the bottle and handed the whiskey back to Flynn.

"You're right, maybe not this year," Flynn said while scratching his beard thoughtfully. "But this spring we're gonna put that bull to work and by next spring we'll have us a good sized herd. And each year, it'll get bigger."

"Uh, huh," Quinn mused, "and where are we gonna get the heifers you planned to breed?"

"Well, the first thing we're gonna do is sell the steers. All they're doin' is eatin' up graze. But the real genius part of this deal is we don't have to buy heifers." Flynn laughed.

"Oh, really," Quinn replied, "we're just gonna go out and pick these heifers off a tree, huh. Or are we gonna start rustlin'." He eyed his brother carefully. "I don't think you need any more of this whiskey. I think you're already drunk."

Flynn took another long pull out of the bottle.

"Hell no!" he shouted. "Wild cattle, brother, wild cattle. This country's full of them."

"You really have lost your mind, brother," Quinn chided. "Just the two of us?"

No, three."

"Three?"

"Yeah, three. Hank's a pretty good hand," Flynn announced proudly. "This will be a family operation."

QUINN, FLYNN, AND Hank spent a couple of months or so building onto the house, the bunk house, and barn. When they weren't building, they were scouring the country to find wild heifers. Before long they had a pretty sizeable herd. They had driven the steers to La Cueva and got a pretty good price; the money would come in handy to buy fencing for a proper corral next to the barn. The men even found store bought dresses for Gwenny and Katie and shirts and trousers for Hank and themselves. With the money Quinn contributed, the family had a fair sized bankroll to enlarge their ranch. Of course, Flynn bought another jug of good Scotch whiskey.

"Gwenny may not be too happy about you buying that jug." Quinn grinned.

"Not to worry, brother. I'll just tell her this whiskey is for medicinal reasons," Flynn replied.

"Yeah." Quinn laughed. "I want to be there when you tell her that."

"I'll give her the dresses first. Then she can't be too mad about the liquor, Quinn," Flynn explained.

"She's your wife; you oughta know her better than I do," Quinn said. "I think you're playing with fire."

"She's alright with an occasional drink . . . as long as I don't get carried away, she's good," Flynn explained.

The three companions rode along in silence for most of the journey home. Each man . . . well two men and a boy . . . was wrapped up in his own thoughts. For his part, Quinn couldn't remember the last time he had felt so at peace. Even alone in the mountains he still felt on edge, agitated, but here with his new family, he was happy. Flynn was happy he could provide for his family and with Quinn and Hank's help, he could build a really fine place to live. Hank was simply awe struck by his new uncle. He respected Flynn and came to love him as a son loves his father, but Quinn was something else again.

"Uncle Quinn, how did you learn to handle horses and cattle the way you do?" Hank asked. "I know Pa has been a buckaroo for a while now and that's how he learned, and taught me, but I thought you studied to be a doctor. Would you mind telling me?"

"Hank, I saw how you handled yourself and your horse on this drive. Obviously, you learned a great deal from your pa. He and I never wanted to be farmers, so every chance we got, we'd take off and work for an old retired cow hand. His name was Charlie and he had been one of the first men we knew who went out west. He raised a nice herd of horses and he taught Flynn and me how to gentle a young horse without fighting him. Your pa caught the frontier fever worse than I did, so the first chance he got, off he went. I knew I didn't want to punch someone else's cows, and I figured I should stay close to home. There wasn't a doctor within twenty miles and since our town needed a doctor, I went to medical school. I had a practice for some years, then the war broke out . . . that was the end of my medical career. And you know the rest. To answer your question, I used what Charlie taught me and added what I learned from a vaquero I met in Colorado. He really could put a handle on a horse without fighting with him."

"Seems to me you must have learned a whole lot because you sure can work a horse," Hank replied.

"Well, thank you, boy." Quinn smiled. "I think I've found my place to raise Apps. Flynn and you can work the cattle and I'll provide you with good cow ponies. Does that sound like a plan?"

"You bet, Uncle Quinn," Hank replied enthusiastically, "and I will get to help, right?"

"I don't see why not." Quinn smiled.

Flynn had been riding ahead kinda wondering to himself how long Quinn would stay and if he'd put his troubles behind him. He heard the loud voices behind him and decided he'd better find out what those two were up to.

"What are you two plotting?" Flynn asked.

"Not much," Quinn replied sheepishly.

"Yeah, I bet," Flynn said knowingly. "Like when we were kids and you talked me into tyin' that piece of string around the neighbor's bull's tail. You said that would prove I was a man. All that deal proved was how stupid gullible I was. Hank, your uncle there was always gettin' me in trouble. Then when I was gettin' a lickin', he was off somewhere's laughin'. So whatcha plannin' now big brother?"

Quinn chuckled at the memory. "Now that I think about that, you were pretty gullible. I could talk you in to just about anything. Seemed you never learned. But this time, Hank and I were talking about how we could get good ranch ponies without spending a dime. We'll raise our own."

"I see." Flynn grinned. "And I suppose my job will be to get the buck out of them."

"Oh, heck no," Quinn assured, "the way I work horses, they don't buck . . ."

The look on Flynn's face said he wasn't convinced.

" . . . no really, I'm telling you the truth. Besides ol Hank here has volunteered to help me out."

Flynn nodded. "Okay, I'll take your word for it, but I think I'll live to regret your plans. I imagine this will come around and bite me in the butt."

"Naw, Flynn," Quinn reassured, "we'll have the best horses in the territory. People will come from miles around to buy our horses."

And true to Quinn's prophecy, people did come to buy his spotted ponies. The Appys the Duncan boys were raising had caught ranchers' eyes. These horses were honest, strong, tough, quick, and agile. Not only that, they were smart. They had the endurance to travel all day in the rough New Mexico territory. They had every quality a man or woman would want in a good horse.

In 1868, the dream the Duncan brothers had, by 1876, grown into one of the most prosperous ranches in Northern New Mexico. Although not the biggest, the Double D Ranch was the most economical. The brothers never wasted anything: they cut spring grass and allowed the hay to dry for winter feed; they never overgrazed a pasture; they never put more stock on a pasture than the graze land would support; and they put in cisterns to catch rain during the wet season for dry spells in summer. What they lacked in quantity, they made up for in quality. There was another unique quality to the Double D: they hired the Jicarilla Apache to work for them. Don't think that didn't raise an eyebrow or two both in town and at Fort Union. Most everybody thought the Duncan clan had lost their minds. But the way Flynn and Quinn figured, better to have Apache as friends rather than enemies. Quinn thought, after all, the Double D was sitting on what used to be Apache land in the first place. They deserved something. The Double D was about the only ranch or farm that didn't have trouble with the Apache. That led people to believe the Duncans were Indian lovers. Of course they wouldn't say that to them directly.

THE BOND WITH the Apache began that summer of '68. Quinn strengthened that bond the following summer when he took a pregnant mare to the Apache village. He hadn't been invited, so the wisdom of the visit was brought into question one evening during supper.

"Brother, are you out of your mind?" Flynn shouted.

Anyone could see the rest of the family had their doubts as well. Katie had become very attached to her new uncle, she was truly frightened that something terrible might happen to him.

"Uncle Quinn," Katie gasped, "the Indians might kill you; you can't go."

She was near to tears. But Quinn, who had found his humanity once again, reassured her, reassured them all.

"Listen, all of you," Quinn reasoned. "The reason I'm going to visit the Apache is to ensure our safety. I plan to broker a treaty between us. One thing I found out with the Cheyenne was that as long as I was honest and treated them fairly, I had a greater chance of keeping my hair. The same is true with the Apache. Besides, I already parlayed with them."

"Since there isn't any way to talk you out of this, I hope they remember that parlay and are still in a friendly mood." Flynn sighed.

"I hope so too," Quinn acknowledged, "but I plan to hedge my bet; I'm going to take a present or two."

"A couple more cows I suppose," Flynn groused.

"Yep," Quinn grinned, "but also I think I'll throw in a little something to sweeten the pot."

Then Quinn turned to Katie.

"Don't you worry, little darlin'," Quinn said softly. "I'll be just fine, you'll see."

The next morning Quinn set out driving a couple cows and leading three Appaloosas: two young colts and a pregnant mare. The Apache telegraph system let them know about his impending arrival long before Quinn reached their camp. One of the young men, wanting to show his bravery, challenged Quinn's intrusion.

"White man trespass on Apache land?" he growled. "You not wanted here."

"I am here to see my brothers Itz-Chu and Jlin-Litzoque,"Quinn declared.

At the mention of the two warriors' names, the young man lost his bravado, but Quinn allowed him to save face.

"I ask you to take me to see my brothers. I have gifts for your chief and your people."

With that, the young warrior took the lead and set off in the direction of the Apache stronghold. About a quarter mile from their camp, Itzu-Chu and Jlin-Litzoque rode out to meet the group.

"My white brother takes chance. To come here uninvited is forbidden," Itz-Chu pronounced.

"With our people there is no reason families cannot visit one another," Quinn stated.

"Almost twelve moons pass. We think Vo`kohe Nan`kohe forget Apache brothers," Jlin-Litzoque replied tersely.

"No, my brothers; I waited for these colts to grow big enough to travel and make sure the mare is bred." Quinn said. "That took time. With these horses, the Apache can raise their own ponies."

"We are warriors not herders," Itz-Chu growled.

"So are the Nez Perce to the north, but they raise great herds of horses and cattle," Quinn countered. "They are not weak."

"We take what we need," growled Jlin-Litzoque.

"Why steal if you don't have to," Quinn countered.

"We not talk now," Itz-Chu said, "we go village."

The small party rode to the village in silence. Quinn couldn't rid a shadow of discomfort. He felt an uncomfortable distance between himself and his brothers. Upon arrival, he was told to wait. Many of the Apache warriors we're painted for war. He wondered why. He hoped he hadn't misjudged their friendship. Quinn waited for what seemed like an eternity when finally Itz-Chu returned with the chief.

"Vo'kohe Nan'kohe," Itz-Chu said, "this is Chief Norroso Taklishim, Grey One. He wise man; can see future."

"I am honored to meet the Chief of the Jicarilla," Quinn replied.

He didn't want to lay his praises on too thick. The Apache, Indians in general, can see through ingenuousness; they hate dishonesty in any form.

"You bring horses and cattle," Norroso Taklishim said. "You want trade with Apache?"

Norroso Taklishim eyed Quinn suspiciously.

"I want nothing in return. I want only for my family and me to live in peace with the Apache," Quinn replied. "I have traded with the Apache before when Itz-Chu and Jlin-Litzoque came to my ranch last year. These horses and cattle are gifts for you and your people. You can raise your own ponies. The bull and heifer could be the beginnings of a cattle herd. If you choose, of course."

Norroso Taklishim looked the horses over carefully. He had a keen eye for good horse flesh.

"You not invited," the chief announced, "white man trespass. Why not we kill you?"

Quinn was getting more uneasy by the minute and his "brother" Itz-Chu wasn't helping any. Finally, Quinn realized his courage was being tested.

"I don't want to fight. I do not fear the Apache. I come here in friendship. I want nothing more than to live alongside my Apache brothers in peace," Quinn repeated. "If the Apache won't welcome me, then I will go. You can keep these horses and cattle as gifts."

Evidently, the stern look on Quinn's face convinced the chief he wanted to be friends, but he'd fight if he had to.

"Vo`kohe Nan`kohe is welcome," Norroso Taklishim said. "These horses good. Get down. We parlay."

Finally, Quinn was reasonably sure he'd keep his hair. Taklishim along with the other tribal leaders talked with Quinn and he was invited to stay the night. He was given his own wickiup which meant he could visit whenever he wished; he'd be welcome. Early the next morning Quinn said his farewells and rode out of the stronghold. Itz-Chu and Jlin-Litzoque accompanied him for a mile or two.

"My brother Vo`kohe Nan`kohe always welcome," Itz-Chu said. Jlin-Litzoque nodded in agreement.

"I am glad there will be no war between us," Quinn replied. "I just wish there could be peace between all Indians and whites."

Quinn was concerned the young men wore war paint. There hadn't been armed conflict between the Jicarilla Apache and the army since 1861. He wondered if he should broach the subject since that might be a sore subject, but what the hell.

"Itz-Chu, I saw young men painted for war, why?"

"White man want all Apache land. Take not ask. Kill women—young ones—elders. No respect," Jlin-Litzoque said angrily. "Don't respect like Vo`kohe Nan`kohe. Men seek yellow iron. Attack village. We kill."

Quinn heard a party of minors had come on Apache land in spite of the treaty. The military figured the reprisal by the Indians was justified, so they let sleeping dogs lie.

"I know," Quinn sighed, "but maybe one day they will. Stay safe, my brothers."

"Stay safe, White Bear," Quinn's Apache brothers said.

Quinn rode away from the stronghold with a renewed sense of hope that one day all Indians and whites would live in peace, but deep down, he knew he was only deluding himself.

Spring of 1876 found the Double D hands busy with branding and doctoring new calves and taking care of newborn foals. Both the cattle and horse herds were growing with each succeeding year and the brothers Duncan we're proud of what they had accomplished in such a short period of time. Hank and Katie were growing into fine young adults; Flynn was found he had taken on the role of the overprotective father. As much as Katie loved Flynn she hated, as she described the situation, being smothered. Gwenny tried to call off the guard dog as she often called Flynn. Gwenny's kind, loving wisdom tempered Flynn's gruff exterior . . . between the two, they made fine parents. Quinn had built himself his own house a mile or so from the main ranch house. His decision was met with a raised eyebrow or two. The way Quinn explained things, the move would keep him from being underfoot all the time. Flynn was afraid Quinn was beginning to get that old wanderlust again. Quinn tried to reassure his younger brother.

"Brother, I'm perfectly happy here," Quinn explained. "I just want my own place so I can work my horses. I don't plan on going anywhere, if that's what you're thinkin'."

"Well, I was wonderin'. At times you get that far off look like you're ready to go explore someplace else," Flynn replied.

"Ya know, brother, this ol boy is just too fat and lazy to go anywhere." Quinn laughed. "Besides, I've gotten used to sleeping on a feather bed. An occasional hunting trip is all the sleeping on the cold, hard ground I want."

The two men sat near the corral, enjoying the evening. They watched the young colt roll on the sandy ground scratching off the sweat after his lesson. Quinn's horses were gathering lots of interest from the local ranchers; they were known as good, hardy cow ponies able to travel in the rough New Mexico country. After a bit, Flynn spoke up about his powerful thirst.

"Quinn, you're my brother and I love you dearly, but you're about the worst host I ever saw."

"Well then, let me apologize, Flynn." Quinn grinned, "What can I do to make up for my bad manners?"

"Would ye be havin' a wee drop of Scotch whiskey in the cupboard?" Flynn asked.

Quinn snorted. "With you, brother, there is no such thing as a wee drop . . . of anything. But, I'll see what I can do."

Quinn went into the house and returned with a bottle filled with amber liquid and two glasses. He looked up and in the distance he could see two mounted Apaches sitting their horses near a grove of junipers. Quinn had talked with the young warriors during his frequent visits to the Apache stronghold. He was curious about what they wanted, but they only watched each other for a bit, then the two young men rode away.

"Flynn, did you see those two Apaches in the junipers just now?" Quinn asked.

"Yeah," Flynn replied. "They have been coming around for the past week or so. They haven't bothered us any, so I didn't bother them. Kukruk and Eskaminzim told me they might want to come work for us, never said one way or the other."

"Maybe we should ask them, 'cause here they come," Quinn observed. "Put the whiskey away, brother."

Flynn threw a saddle pad over the scotch and the two men walked toward the young warriors to have a friendly chat. Quinn welcomed the two young men and invited them to step down and parlay.

"My brother, Flynn, and I welcomed you to our home. Please sit down and we'll smoke and talk," Quinn said amiably. "Neighbors should visit from time to time. You have welcomed me to your home; now I welcome you to ours."

The two Apache walked over to where Quinn pointed and sat down. As he had done many times before, he went into the house and retrieved his ceremonial pipe and tobacco. The two young men introduced themselves; the older of the two did more of the talking.

"I am Nitis, Friend," he said and pointed to his companion. "My brother, Tarak, Star."

The four men shook hands and Quinn passed the pipe to Nitis, then to Tarak, then to Flynn, and finally he took a long draw on the pipe.

"What brings you to our home?" Quinn asked, then added. "You are welcome anytime for no reason, but since you have never come before, I can only think there must be a special reason."

"Yes," Nitis said. "Chief Norroso Taklishim sent us. We bring message."

He nodded to his brother who went to his horse and returned with a talisman from the Chiricahua Apache.

"Chief say trouble come," Tarak said. "Victorio prepare for war."

"Big medicine Cheyenne country," Nitis added. "Yellow Hair Custer dead. Cheyenne and Sioux kill. Bring back buffalo."

After the spring work was finished, the family had gone into La Cueva for a little celebration. The Duncan brothers had heard there was trouble brewing from punchers who came south from Montana, Colorado, and Wyoming. The

Sioux were just a might peeved that miners had come into the Black Hills looking for gold. They had signed a treaty, for all the good that did. As usual, the government ignored what they promised and let miners and settlers come on to sacred Lakota land to take whatever they wanted. Whites killed off the buffalo, hoping to starve the Indians into capitulation; all that did was make them good and mad. The Sioux and Cheyenne quit quarreling between themselves and beat the hell out of Custer and the 7th Calvary on June 26, 1876. Unfortunately, that victory would spell the end of the Sioux and Cheyenne. Sitting Bull headed for Canada and the rest of the Cheyenne and Sioux hightailed out of the country. But in the meantime, the news traveled south and the Apache were emboldened for a good fight with any and all whites who came onto Apache land. Shamans in every band and clan were doing the Ghost Dance stirring up trouble. The Jicarilla Apache had been good neighbors after the end of their war, most everyone in town and on farms and ranches near Fort Union traded with them. Still, blood is thicker than water; the Jicarilla might feel some obligation to aid their Chiricahua, Mescalero, and White Mountain brothers if they went to war. If there was any trouble, more than likely the army would overreact and there would be a full scale war as a result. Victorio and Cochise were reasonable, but Geronimo . . . well, that was a whole 'nother story.

"What does Norroso Taklishim want from us? We will do whatever we can to keep the peace and honor our Apache brothers," Quinn said.

Flynn nodded in agreement.

"We don't want any trouble. Your Apache brothers work for us and we appreciate all the Apache have given us. You are our family."

"Apache feel same," Tarak said. "Duncans honest. Great warriors. Treat Apache with respect. Chief want Duncan brothers come for parlay. Decide join Mescalero and Chiricahua brothers in war, maybe."

"I would hate to see my Apache brothers go to war for any reason," Quinn said. "Flynn and I will come to your stronghold for a parlay. We'll get our gear and saddle up.

Gwenny always had a big jar filled with cookies. They became a favorite treat when the Apache came to visit and it was a damn sight safer than giving them whiskey.

"Flynn squaw have cookies, maybe?" Tarak asked.

Gwenny heard the two braves ride in and she was prepared . . . cold milk and cookies.

"You bet, Tarak," Gwenny said. She came out of the house with a platter filled with cookies and a gallon jug of milk.

"Here," she said and placed the goodies on a table under the "parlay tree." "Eat and drink your fill. I've put some in a sack to take back to share with everyone in the village."

She looked from one, then the other.

"Now, make sure you don't eat them all on the way home," she said sternly. "Promise me."

"We give word to Duncan's woman. No eat all," Nitis promised.

Gwenny handed Flynn saddle bags filled with food and Flynn reached down and gave her a kiss.

"What's this?" Flynn asked. "The Apache will feed us well."

"I know," Gwenny said, "But the last time you went to visit, you over ate Apache stew and got sick. I don't want you to make the same mistake on this trip. How long do you think you'll be gone?"

"Shouldn't be more than a week or ten days," Flynn said. "Ol Hank there will look after things, right son?"

Hank had grown into a fine man. Now twenty-three, Flynn and Quinn made Hank a full partner in the ranch and he was expected to do what was required of a partner. He learned to handle cattle and horses, but more importantly, he had learned to handle men. The hands respected Hank because he didn't expect the men to do anything he wouldn't. Quinn and Flynn didn't just give Hank a partnership, he earned his place in the business over the past eight years.

"Sure, Pa," Hank replied. "You don't have to worry; I'll take care of things."

"I know you will son," Flynn said confidently.

Not to be left out, Katie entered the conversation. At sixteen, Katie was a beautiful young woman. She looked very much like her mother . . . in fact Gwenny often said Katie looked just like her when she was sixteen.

"What about me?" Katie asked indignantly.

"Yes?" Quinn raised an eyebrow. "What about you?"

Quinn and Katie had a special relationship. He loved her as if she were his own. They spent much time together and Quinn taught her everything he knew about horses and cattle and how to defend herself. She was a crack shot with both a Colt pistol and a Winchester rifle. Katie reciprocated in kind. She taught Quinn how to trust in his fellow man again. She taught him to hope and she taught him to see the beauty around him in all things.

"Well," she said. "I can do just about everything around here as well as Hank can. Plus I can keep this ranch from going into debt. I keep the books all up to date and proper. Hank can barely add four and four."

"Hey," Hank retorted. "I can so do my sums and read. I can play the fiddle too. I don't see you making music 'round here, missy."

"All right you two," Gwenny said softly. "I think we can all agree you are both talented in your own way and we all love you equally."

The men chuckled and shook their heads and rode off to the northwest and the Jicarilla stronghold.

"Ya know, Flynn." Quinn smiled thoughtfully. "One of these days there's gonna be a role reversal on the ranch. Those two children are gonna take over and we'll be taking orders from them."

"Don't think I don't know that brother." Flynn laughed. "But ya know I couldn't be more proud of those two. I know that the ranch will be in good hands when we're gone."

"Brother," Quinn grinned, "I hope you don't mind if the impending takeover waits for a long spell. I'm not ready for the rockin' chair just yet."

"Yeah," Flynn agreed, "me either."

The Jicarilla stronghold was a good two day ride, but considering the urgency of the parlay the four riders pushed on well into the night. Generally, riding into an Apache camp after sundown wasn't a good idea, the two white men figured they were safe enough with the two young warriors leading the way. As usual, their arrival was known long before they got within eye or earshot of the village. Riders were sent out to escort the Duncan brothers into the stronghold. Chief Norroso Taklishim greeted them; he was flanked by Itz-Chu and Jlin-Litzoque.

"The Duncan brothers welcome," Taklishim said tersely. "We talk morning."

And that was that. The chief turned and walked into his wickiup for the night. The Apache brothers were a little more welcoming.

"My brother and me glad to see white brothers," Itz-Chu said. Jlin-Litzoque nodded in agreement.

"Yes, my brothers," Quinn said. "We haven't seen each other for too long."

The Apache brothers and even Flynn smiled knowingly. Jlin-Litzoque got right to the point.

"White Bear miss Dahteste not Apache brothers."

"Now that just isn't so," Quinn protested . . . rather weakly. "I have missed visiting my Apaches brothers. Well, the whole family, even."

At this, the three men laughed heartily at Quinn's discomfort.

"All right, I'll admit, I have missed Dahteste." Quinn looked around furtively. "Ummm, she wouldn't happen to still be up, would she?"

Itz-Chu and Jlin-Litzoque looked at each other; they wore the kind of look only protective big brothers would wear when prospective suitors came nosing around their sister.

"Boys," Flynn snickered, "ya might as well let him go visit Dahteste. We can always hang him by his ears if he gets too forward."

"Oh well thanks, lil brother." Quinn sneered. "Nice to know my brother will stand up for me in a pinch."

"What do you expect," Flynn said flatly, "I'm a father too ya know."

Quinn shook his head and marched off in the direction of Dahteste's parents' wickiup. Quinn had been smitten with the Apache woman since the first time he saw her. She was older than what would be considered a maiden and her husband had been killed in a buffalo hunt three years previously. Her parents had yet to choose another husband for her. But she was a handsome maid and her bride price wasn't anything to joke about . . . ten ponies and five saddles. Not many Apache men had that kind of wealth or they figured the price was too high, or both. Quinn didn't care; he'd pay that much and more if Dahteste would have him. And he didn't care about the barriers between their two races; he'd do whatever was necessary to make this woman happy. For her part, Dahteste meant Woman Warrior and she was not a woman to be trifled with and she let Quinn know in no uncertain terms.

"Good evening, Dahteste," Quinn said. "I have missed you."

"Quinn speaks falsely," the woman said. "I have not seen White Bear for two moons. Should have come sooner."

"That's true, Dahteste," Quinn apologized, "but work at the ranch has kept me at home. This is a busy time of year. But believe me, I have missed you. Each night I look at the moon and stars; I think their beauty can't compare to yours. I pray to the North Star each night that, one day, you will be my wife. If that too is your wish, I will ask your parents . . . tonight even."

There, he spoke his piece. His heart was in this throat. Imagine, a man his size and age being brought to his knees by a little slip of a woman. Dahteste looked into Quinn's eyes looking for any sign of deceit; she could find nothing but love.

"I have been afraid. Afraid you would find another. I am afraid no longer," Dahteste whispered. "I will become your wife."

Knock me over with a feather, Quinn thought; I never thought this would happen to me. I'll be damned.

THE JICARILLA APACHES decided not to join their Apache cousins in this fight. The parlay to which the Duncan brothers were invited ended with Chief Norroso Taklishim deciding to stay on their land and mind their own business. The best part of that, as far as Quinn was concerned, meant that he and Dahteste could get married.

"Do I really have to get all fixed up like this?" Quinn whined.

"Just stop fussing, Uncle Quinn," Katie ordered. "You have to be presentable for your wedding."

Flynn was thoroughly enjoying his brother's discomfort.

"Why brother you look plumb handsome." Flynn laughed. "I'd hardly recognize you."

"Very funny," Quinn said sarcastically. "One day I will repay you believe me."

He squirmed and tugged at the tight collar choking him. Gwenny continued to fuss and brush Quinn's buckskin jacket. Hank was spit polishing the bridegroom's new boots.

Katie was charged with trimming Quinn's hair, mustache, and goatee. Finally, everything was judged satisfactory and Quinn's torture was over. Soon, he would see all the unwanted attention was worth the trouble. At the sight of Dahteste, Quinn went weak in the knees; at the last moment, Flynn and Hank grabbed hold of the nervous bridegroom to keep from falling on his face. Brides are usually very beautiful, but Dahteste was breathtaking. She wore a white deerskin dress with turquoise beading; in her raven black hair, she wore a single eagle feather, and her dark eyes sparkled in the firelight.

The proceedings were about to begin. Itz-Chu and Jlin-Litzoque, the bride's brothers, escorted Quinn to stand next to Dahteste and before the holy man, Wicasa Sani, Sage Old One. From this point on, whatever was said was lost on Quinn. He was so transfixed on his new bride, he was aware of nothing else. Finally, he was brought to attention by a sharp slap to the back of his head.

Itz-Chu whispered, "White Bear time answer Wicasa Sani."

"I promise to love and protect Dahteste for as long as I live," Quinn whispered.

Next the shaman repeated the question to Dahteste.

"You will protect and love White Bear long as you live?"

"I promise also," Dahteste replied quietly.

"Go then live in wickiup as man and wife for long as you live," Wicasa Sani commanded.

And that as they say is that. An Apache wedding ceremony is short. What is important is the life the couple leads together. Quinn and Dahteste rode together to their wickiup a mile or so away from the main encampment. When the time was right, they would move their living quarters within the confines of the main camp. For now, however, the couple would be given privacy any young couple should receive. As for the rest of the tribe and Quinn's family, this was an occasion for celebrating and celebrate they did. There was singing, dancing, and feasting. Flynn, Gwenny, Katie, and Hank were welcomed into Dahteste's family . . . this was just how things were done. And there was the small matter of the bride price . . . Quinn had already given the family ten head of his finest Appys and saddles. Flynn wanted to make sure they were all going to live in peace, so in addition to the horses, he offered ten head of cattle: a bull and nine heifers. Itz-chu and his family accepted with much fanfare, exclaiming the Duncans were honest and " . . . had much integrity . . ." no small thing coming from an Apache. The newly married couple were not seen or heard from for over a month. When they finally made an appearance in the stronghold, Quinn's new brothers-in-law couldn't resist giving Quinn the business, Apache style.

"White Bear finally tired." Jlin-Litzoque chuckled.

Itz-chu looked at his brother.

"White Bear look to have many children before too old."

Both brothers doubled over in laughter at Quinn's expense.

"All right," Quinn scolded. "I notice neither of you are married and have children."

"We too busy. Must protect whole tribe. No time for wife. That come later," Jlin-Litzoque retorted.

"Now must talk. Chief need White Bear help."

"Whatever I can do, I will," Quinn promised.

Chief Norroso Taklishim wanted Quinn to accompany him and a delegation of Apache elders to Fort Union to relay their intentions to stay out of the Chiricahua Apache war. The Jicarilla Apache had long ago separated from their Apache cousins to the south and quite frankly were a bit miffed when the Chiricahua didn't come to their aid fifteen years earlier when they fought the US Army. They felt no obligation to get mixed up in someone else's fight and they wanted to make sure the army understood that and there would be no reprisals simply because they were Apache as well. Colonel Harmon reassured the delegation there would be nothing to worry about as long as there were no fighting here. Quinn wanted to know just what that meant.

"Listen, Colonel Harmon." Quinn scowled menacingly. "I warn you, if there is any trouble, the Jicarilla won't be the cause of the problem. But I guarantee they will finish it and we Duncans will be right 'long side of them . . . and so will there be all the ranchers and settlers around here."

"Mr. Duncan," the Colonel replied, trying to sound brave. "Are you threatening the United States Army?"

"Colonel, obviously, you weren't listening closely enough," Quinn said in a low, dangerous voice. "I'm not threatening you; I'm saying flat out. Don't start something you can't finish."

Quinn turn to the Apaches he had come with.

"We are done here. Let's go home. Good day, Colonel."

THREE YEARS PASSED; three years filled with raids and confrontation. Finally, the lid blew off in April, 1879. Victorio led his Chiricahua Apaches in a last ditch effort to rid Apache lands of whites. In the Alma Massacre and siege of Fort Tularosa, Victorio attacked and killed forty-one settlers and stole forty-six horses. Dubbed Victorio's War, from 1879-1880, the Apache raided farms and ranches, killed settlers and miners, and stole horses. He outfought the 5th, 9th, and 10th divisions of cavalry by using guerilla tactics of ambush, then fleeing into the mountains. But finally, on April 14, 1880, the Mexican army caught up with Victorio in the Tres Castillos Mountains in Mexico. The Apache chief along with sixty warriors and eighteen women and children were killed; sixty-eight women and children were taken prisoner. Thus, the end of Victorio's War. Up north, there was tension between the Jicarilla and the army, but no open hostilities and once the Victorio's Chiricahuas were subdued, only Geronimo remained. He too finally surrendered in 1886. That was the end of the Apache wars in the Southwest.

Although the Duncan brothers understood the reason why the Apache fought for so long and so hard, how could they condone the savagery with which the Apache fought? Yes, the argument could be made, whites had done barbarous things as well. But killing, mutilating, raping women and children as far as Flynn was concerned, that was beyond the pale. Quinn, on the other hand, had seen how inhuman men could be to each other and simply wrote the whole thing off to man's inhumanity to man. He saw that first hand during the war. Rich white men keeping other men slaves for no other reason than the color of their skin. He found himself rather ambivalent to the whole mess. At any rate, the wars were over and he could concentrate on raising a family and building the ranch.

In the four and a half years since their marriage, Dahteste had presented Quinn with two baby boys and was carrying a third child. However, pregnancy and caring for three babies didn't keep Dahteste from working right alongside Quinn. She was a quick study and had learned a good deal about working with cattle. As for riding, Apaches, men and women, were noted the best riders in the Southwest. She especially liked working with the young horses and Quinn let her " . . . have at it" as he would say. For Quinn, this was the happiest time of his life, but he couldn't shake a feeling of foreboding. He often spoke about this with Flynn. Of course, Flynn was no help. He'd just say Quinn was looking for trouble or couldn't stand prosperity. Finally, he thought he'd go talk to the smartest member of Flynn's family.

"Hello, Gwenny," Quinn said as he rode up.

Gwenny was working in the flower garden. People came from miles around to admire her green thumb.

"Well, hello yourself, Quinn." Gwenny smiled. "What brings you up here in the middle of the day? Shouldn't you be out tending cows or riding broncs?"

"Perhaps I should be, Gwenny," Quinn grinned, "but there's something I'd like to talk to you about. My thick headed brother doesn't seem to understand my problem. I was hoping you might."

"Of course, Quinn," his sister-in-law replied, "what's wrong?"

"I'm not sure. I haven't been this happy in my entire life. I have a beautiful wife and two fine boys and another child on the way. I have an extended family, you and your kids, and Flynn. The Apache have accepted our marriage. I have a ranch, I'm doing what I have wanted to do for a very long time. I have no idea what's wrong except that I just can't shake this feeling something bad is going to happen. Crazy, huh."

Gwenny shook her head. "No, not crazy, confused maybe, apprehensive, probably. If I were you, with the connections you have with the Apache, I would go see Itz-Chu. He can help you more than I can."

Oddly enough, that made sense, but something he had never thought of before. If anything could help him understand what he was feeling, Native American mysticism could.

"That's a good idea." Quinn beamed. "I don't know why I never thought of that before. Thank you Gwenny."

"You don't need to thank me, Quinn." Gwenny smiled. "That's what families do . . . help each other."

I just hope Flynn understands how lucky he is, Quinn thought. He walked up the road that ran between the two ranches about half a mile or so. He felt as though a heavy weight had been lifted from his shoulders. While he still felt somewhat apprehensive, the sense of foreboding was gone. He walked around to the back door and found Dahteste hanging laundry on the line. The two boys, one and two years old, were playing on a blanket nearby. Dahteste was nearing her time and Quinn hated to see her working so hard.

"Why does Quinn's woman refuse to mind him and not work so hard? Woman you must obey your husband," Quinn said, trying to be serious, but failing miserably.

Dahteste couldn't help but laugh.

"Are you going to beat me if I do not obey you, my husband?" Dahteste giggled.

Quinn sighed audibly. "Dahteste, I just don't want you to overdo. You are so close to your due date. Katie has offered to come help you do chores. Why don't you let her help?"

"Katie has her own chores to do," Dahteste reasoned. "I rest when I get tired. Stop worrying. Come sit with me and the boys, here, in the shade. Tell me what Gwenny advised you to do about your worrying."

Quinn raised an eyebrow and cleared his throat. "To what worrying might you be referring?"

"Don't play with me. I know my husband too well not to know when he is worried," Dahteste replied.

AGAIN QUINN LET out a sigh.

"I've just got a lot on my mind lately and I haven't been able to figure out what's going on, that's all."

"And you didn't think to talk to your wife about this?" Dahteste asked.

"I didn't want you to worry," Quinn replied.

"And you think I would worry less when you don't confide in me?" Dahteste questioned.

"I'm sorry; I forget you know me better than I know myself." Quinn smiled. They walked over to what had come to be known as the parlay tree and sat down on a buffalo robe.

"You might think this sounds strange," Quinn began, "but I guess I can't stand prosperity. I have this terrible feeling I can't shake that something terrible is going to happen—something I have no control over. Crazy, huh?"

Dahteste studied Quinn's face carefully; a face she knew so well. She knew every line, crease, and scar and how each was made. Even with all that, she couldn't unravel the foreboding Quinn carried. She gently caressed Quinn's face. She traced over every mark with her finger.

"My husband, I am here to help you shoulder all the burdens you carry," Dahteste whispered, "but I can't help you on this journey. You must carry this weight yourself. Go to the shaman; he will heal your troubled spirit."

"I will go to the wise man of the Apache," Quinn said thoughtfully. Wicaso Sani, Sage Old One, will prepare me for my journey. But I worry about you; the baby will come soon. I want you to go stay with Gwenny and Flynn. Then I won't worry . . . as much anyway."

Dahteste started to speak a word of protest, but wasn't able to utter a sound. With a wave of his hand Quinn stopped any further discussion.

"I won't change my mind; you're going to Flynn's place and that's final."

"WOULD YOU STOP worrying," Flynn admonished. "We will take good care of your wife. Worry about yourself."

Dahteste studied her husband's demeanor carefully before she spoke.

"My husband, you will worry about me whether I am here or home. There is no need. Flynn is right. Take care of yourself." Dahteste smiled.

Quinn leaned down from the saddle and kissed his wife tenderly. "Yes wife, I will."

The ride to the Apache stronghold was uneventful. Now, since his marriage, this place was his second home. The people here were his extended family so the fact that he had been watched long before he reached the stronghold was of no concern. He looked up to see his brother-in-law approaching.

"Welcome, my brother," Itz-Chu said. "You come alone. Is something wrong with Dahteste?"

"Thank you, brother," Quinn replied. "There is nothing wrong. Dahteste is nearing her time and I don't want her to travel. She stays with Flynn and his family where she will be safe. I come for the spirit healing. I come to see Wicaso Sani, the shaman. My spirit is sick and needs to be healed."

"Then good White Bear come. Wise one heal my brother," Itz-Chu said confidently.

The ritual of healing is a sacred affair with the Apache, as with all Native tribes, and is part of their religion. Suffice to say, the supplicant asks the Shaman to help him purge all the impurities from his body so his spirit may be healed. The Shaman chants prayers specific to the ritual while the supplicant goes into the sweat hut. There was a certain amount of peyote Quinn had to smoke while the ritual was taking place. He wasn't allowed to eat or drink anything for the duration of the ritual. Given all these circumstances, Quinn would undoubtedly have hallucinations, which was the point. The Apache believed the supplicant was communicating with the Great Spirit through the vision. He would tell Quinn what he must do to heal. Some sort of quest would more than likely be involved.

After three days, Quinn regained consciousness in Itz-Chu's wickiup. He had been in the wickiup for four days without food or water. Obviously, there was a real danger of dying from dehydration and Quinn was close to that. He had seen his vision in the nick of time so he could get out of the hut and be tended to. For the moment, Quinn was dazed and confused. He opened his eyes and tried to focus.

"How long have I been out?" Quinn asked.

"Four suns come and go," Jlin-Litzoque said. "Worry White Bear die."

"No not die," Itz-Chu interjected. "White Bear strong."

Quinn tried to sit up with varying degrees of success.

"Oh my God," Quinn groaned, "what hit me? My head feels like I been beat with a club."

"White Bear sick from peyote." Jlin-Litzoque laughed. "Sacred weed strong. Bring White Bear to knees."

Quinn felt miserable enough without having being chided by his brother-in-law.

"Very funny," Quinn moaned. "But what I wouldn't give for a good stout cup of Flynn's coffee."

The wickiup he wound up in belonged to he and Dahteste and he had left a supply of coffee, jerked beef, and parched corn. Hopefully, the coffee was still there. Then, like manna from heaven, he detected the aroma of hot coffee.

Itz-Chu handed the hot beverage to Quinn and smiled. "This strong drink. Warriors drink before hunt. Gives strength. Takes sleep away night."

"My brother, I could kiss you!" Quinn exclaimed.

Itz-Chu didn't know what to make of that remark, and he just backed up a bit. Quinn drank the black elixir with gusto and asked for a refill. The second cup he drank slowly savoring every sip.

"That's better," Quinn declared, "I feel almost human again. I think I could eat now. My backbone is rubbing a hole in my stomach."

As if on cue, Quinn's mother-in-law entered the wickiup carrying a plate of venison . . . a very big plate.

"My son hungry after sweat," said Liluye, Hawk Singing, "must eat."

"Thank you, mother," Quinn replied. "I could eat a horse."

Liluye looked at Quinn quizzically.

"Venison," the woman said. "Want horse, I fix."

"No, no, Liluye. That is just a white man's expression. Venison is just fine; thank you very much," Quinn said.

Quinn ate as though he had a hollow leg. He devoured the food like a condemned man eating his last meal. In the blink of an eye, the food was gone and he was looking for more.

"That was very tasty, Liluye." Quinn beamed. "I'd like to have some more please."

"No not good eat too much . . . get sick . . . eat more later." his mother-in-law said sternly.

"But I'm still hungry," Quinn pleaded, but to no avail.

"Later. Get more," Liluye declared as she walked away.

'Dang," Quinn observed, "she's a stubborn woman."

"Chew tree bark," Itz-Chu said and handed Quinn a piece of dried bark.

"You're serious?" Quinn asked incredulously.

"Keep stomach good. Not get sick," Jlin-Litzoque said.

Reluctantly, Quinn took the bark and bit off a piece. Slowly the corners of Quinn's mouth turned up in a slight smile.

"Hmmm, not too bad," Quinn announced.

Quinn rested for most of the day and walked around the encampment visiting with family and friends. He was soaking up the Apache culture like a thirsty man drinks water. There was a reason for everything the Apache did; they were one with the earth. They firmly believed the earth was their mother and the Creator put them here to be caretakers of the land, water, plants, and animals. Mother Earth was sacred and the elders had a duty to teach the younger generation to care for Her as well. They understood to abuse the earth would mean they would suffer as well. Quinn came upon an old man and woman sitting in the shade holding hands. He started to speak to them when he felt a soft touch on this shoulder.

"White Bear not speak."

Quinn turned at Liluye's voice.

"Old ones dying," she continued. "Come, we talk."

Liluye explained that the couple had been together as long as anyone could remember . . . fifty years maybe. They came from the White Mountain tribe down south. They journeyed here many years ago to get away from the fighting with the neighboring tribes. Their children were killed by white miners. They had nothing left themselves. They should be left alone to await death together. This was a sacred time for them and the rest of the tribe would respect their wishes. After their deaths, they would be given the sacred burial rites. The people would pay their respects in a formal celebration of their lives. Soon the old ones would begin their death song; death would come soon after.

Quinn shook his head; there was much about the Apache way of life he didn't understand. Their views about life and death for one. Still, the more he thought about the old couple, he was able to reconcile their beliefs. They had lived a long time and had lost so much; somehow they had the right to decide how they would leave this world...that made sense. The more time he spent with his extended family, the more the feeling of foreboding that had been weighing him down lessened. Still, the feeling he had to take a journey wouldn't leave him. He said as much to Itz-Chu.

"My brother, I feel much better, but I think my journey is yet unfinished," Quinn explained. "This may sound crazy, but an inner voice is speaking to me saying I must travel to a high place where my life will be spread before my eyes. Do you know of such a place?"

Itz-Chu nodded and motioned for Quinn to follow him.

Itz-Chu led Quinn through a grove of junipers and up a slight incline to a knoll not far from the village. He pointed to a high mesa some twenty miles to the west.

"White Bear go there. Find self," he said.

"That sounds simple enough," Quinn surmised.

"No," Itz-Chu said forcefully, "Not simple. White Bear heart be pure. Sweat, fast first."

Quinn was confused.

"I thought I already did that."

"Quinn sweat poison out of body," Itz-Chu pointed out. "Now sweat poison from spirit."

"All right," Quinn sighed, "whatever I must do, I will."

Once Quinn had finished all the rituals to purify mind and body, he packed up and rode the twenty miles to the distant mesa. Upon arrival, he found the trail to the top was impassable except on foot. He unsaddled his horse and left him to graze; where hopefully he would still be when he was ready to leave. Damnation, he thought, why does the Great Spirit or whomever make things so difficult? On the other hand, if this journey was easy, then maybe the result wouldn't be satisfactory. Oh well.

Quinn began the difficult climb which took the better part of the day. The sun was beginning its descent below the horizon by the time Quinn climbed over the last ledge. The Creator had left His handprint all over the land. The fading sun cast long shadows across the red clay deposits, green grass, and sage in the valley below. There couldn't be a sight any more beautiful anywhere. Well, there was nothing to do now but settle in for the night . . . he had no idea what to expect.

Quinn fell asleep in no time. The climb up the mesa had taken a toll on his already compromised system. He had no idea what time, but he dreamed. The dream was a disjointed series of visions from his life. Some pleasant, some not so much. One vision in particular kept repeating . . . that must mean something important . . . again and again. He was on the Gettysburg battlefield and in the distance he could make out the figures of his wife and children. A rebel soldier had them in his sights and was about to pull the trigger. Dahteste couldn't see the soldier, nor could she hear Quinn shouting for her to get down. In his present position, he couldn't move. To make matters worse, he had run out of ammunition in his rifle and the rebel was out range for his revolver to do any good. As though he had been given divine intervention, a dead soldier's rifle was just a few yards away . . . and as luck would have it, the rifle was a repeater. If only he could cover the twenty yards, without getting killed, and the rifle still had bullets. There were too many ifs, but he had no choice. In a mad dash, Quinn plunged forward, rolled, and picked up the rifle in one smooth motion. He came to his feet, aimed, and fired. The force of the bullets striking the Johnny Reb sent him reeling. He landed at Dahteste's feet, eyes open, and the vacant expression of the dead on his face. At that point, everything on the battlefield stopped. There wasn't a sound; only Dahteste, the little boys, and he were left alive surrounded by the dead. Quinn woke up covered in a cold sweat. Was this dream a warning? If so, what did Gettysburg and Dahteste have in common? He could make no sense of this. What the hell did this dream mean? Perhaps Wicaso Sani could help unravel the mystery.

"WHITE MAN WAR not over," the Shaman stated. "White Bear still fight here."

Wicaso Sani pointed to Quinn's head. Quinn shook his head.

The old man elaborated. "White Bear leave. Soldiers still fight. Go back, finish fight."

Oh hell no! Quinn thought. There is no way in the world he was going back East. But where does Dahteste fit in the vision? he wondered.

"What happen White Bear happen family," Wicaso Sani explained.

Quinn was stunned. This realization was like a hard slap in the face. But who wants her dead? An Apache hating settler? Somebody who has a grudge against him? Someone in town? Who must be kill to save his wife? He never saw the soldier's face clearly. And what about his sons? They weren't more than babies. All way home, Quinn tried to puzzle out the meaning of the vision. The home ranch gate was a welcoming sight indeed. The short ride to Flynn's place seemed to take an eternity. The children playing out front and two women on the front porch was a beautiful picture indeed.

"Children, look up. See who comes." Dahteste smiled.

The toddler's wallered to their hands and feet then waddled off toward their father. Quinn urged his horse forward and swept up the two boys in his arms. The boys' laughter could not be contained.

"Faster papa, faster," the older of the two lads shouted.

"Just how fast do you want to go?" Quinn laughed.

"Like the wind, papa."

Quinn spurred his horse to a gallop and when he reached the porch, he sat the stallion down to a sliding stop.

"Well, that was quite an arrival." Gwenny laughed.

"Stir up much dust," Dahteste observed. "Husband should be careful with sons."

Oops, Quinn thought. Someone is still miserably pregnant. At least she waited until I got home. He leapt from the saddle, still holding onto his boys, and wrapped his arms around his wife in a very strong bear hug. Not without protest from his sons.

"Papa, you're squishing us," Conner cried out.

"Oh, sorry 'bout that." Quinn chuckled.

Reluctantly he released his wife long enough to sit the boys down. They had all the family togetherness they wanted and ran off to play. Quinn couldn't help but smile at his sons. Dahteste and they were the pride and joy of his life; he couldn't imagine life without them. He returned his attention to his wife. Gently, he placed his hands on her distended belly. He felt the baby kick.

"This child hurry to see father." Dahteste smiled.

"The feeling is mutual. I'm anxious to see our child," Quinn said softly.

For such a huge man, Quinn could be surprisingly soft and tender. However, if provoked, he could be a tenacious, ruthless, and vicious adversary. He had a wry sense of humor and was just as quick with a joke as he was drawing his Colt 45. Dahteste was a good match for Quinn. She brought out Quinn's softer side, but she too could be a worthy opponent. She could ride and shoot as well as any man, perhaps better.

She had lethal skills with a Bowie knife and a bow and arrow as well. They both took a hand in raising their sons. There wasn't anything either one wouldn't do for their children. One might say they were the perfect couple.

"I just wish the child would come soon." Quinn sighed. "And I bet you are tired of carrying him around, too."

"Yes, husband. But my time close," Dahteste responded.

Fortunately for everyone concerned, Quinn was still a doctor and he learned Apache healing skills as well. His wife and everyone in the family was in good hands if a doctor's skills were needed . . . and needed they would be that very night. Almost to the day of their marriage, June 23, 1881, Dahteste went into labor.

The couple enjoyed the cool nights so they had taken to sleeping outside in a grove of junipers near the house. The boys were bundled up near a campfire sound asleep. Quinn was snoring away as usual. Deep into the night, Quinn was awakened by a firm shake on his shoulder.

"Quinn, Quinn are you awake?" Dahteste asked.

"Huh, what?" Quinn replied sleepily.

"Quinn, the child comes, now!" his wife declared.

"Yes, I'm up, I'm up," Quinn said. "How far apart are the contractions? Do they come quick or slow?"

"Quick. This child come fast," Dahteste panted.

"All right, don't worry, I'm with you," Quinn whispered.

Quickly, he threw more wood on the fire and walked a few steps to his medical supplies cached nearby. He went to the well and filled a large cooking pot with water, which he placed on the fire. Then he sent Rufus to get Gwenny and Katie . . . Flynn (he knew from experience) would be of no help at all.

"Rufus, go find Gwenny and Katie," Quinn commanded. "Bring them here, boy."

The big dog ran off in the direction of Flynn's house, barking with every step. If that didn't wake up the household, nothing would. Immediately, Quinn turned his attention back to Dahteste. He gently wiped her face with a wet towel. He also dipped into his medical bag and took out a pinch of peyote.

"Here, wife, chew this. The peyote will ease your pain. I want you to take deep, regular breaths and let them out slowly. Later, I will tell you when to pant."

Dahteste tried to smile, but a strong contraction hit. She squeezed Quinn's hand hard enough to make him wince.

"Is my grip too strong, my husband?" Dahteste gasped.

"No, grip as hard as you need to; I'm strong enough to withstand a little pinch. Rest now." Quinn smiled.

The couple settled down to await the impending birth of their child. The contractions leveled off and were regularly spaced. A good amount of time would pass before she would deliver. I wish babies were born as quick as foals were, Quinn thought, and with a whole lot less trouble. He continued to swab his wife's face and tried to make her as comfortable as possible. Pretty quick, he heard Rufus, Gwenny, Katie, and Flynn hurrying toward them.

"I'm glad you're here. Good boy, Rufus," Quinn said.

"You're welcome, Quinn. We're here to help, but you're the doctor; you tell us what to do," Gwenny said.

"Well, now we're just waiting. I gave her a little pinch of peyote to ease the pain. She's resting now. Umm, I do have one question; uh, why did you bring him?"

Quinn cocked his head toward his brother. "You know he's pretty much worthless."

"I heard that, brother," Flynn said slightly offended. "I am capable of tending the fire and carrying water while you and Gwenny tend to your wife."

"I'm sorry, Flynn," Quinn apologized, "but I saw how you acted when your mare foaled. You were frozen in your tracts."

"Jeez, Quinn," Flynn protested, "that was thirty years ago; I was just a kid."

"Flynn, a leopard never changes his spots," Quinn countered.

"Well I ain't no leopard," Flynn argued.

Gwenny had had enough of the brothers' conversation. "Would you two stop? We have more important things to do right now!"

"You're right," Quinn said, "I'm sorry. Dahteste, how are you feeling? How far apart are the contractions?"

"They are close together. I think the baby comes," Dahteste gasped.

Quinn moved between her legs to prepare for the delivery.

"I think you're right. I can see the baby's head. Gwenny, help Dahteste sit up slightly; that way she will be able to push better. When you feel a contraction, push as hard as you can and pant quickly. Flynn keep the water hot," Quinn said.

Dahteste must have been in severe pain but she never cried out. She pushed when Quinn instructed and before too long, the baby came into the world . . . another strong boy. Although the Apache woman never cried out, there was an obvious look of relief on her face. Her breath had returned to normal almost immediately after her child's birth, a testament to her physical endurance. There's one thing to be a proud father, but quite another kind of pride when a father assists his wife in the delivery of their child. Quinn was near to bursting with pride and love . . . and that showed on his face.

"Is my husband pleased with our child," Dahteste asked.

Quinn bundled the child up in a blanket Gwenny handed to him. Then motioned to Flynn to vacate the premises. Of course Flynn was a little slow on the uptake.

"What?" Flynn asked, "aren't we gonna stay . . ." Gwenny cut him off and dragged him away.

"They should be alone," Gwenny admonished. "This is a private time for them; they don't need us right now. We can see the baby later."

The couple didn't notice Flynn and his family had left . . . they were in a world of their own creation . . . theirs and the Creator. The little boy was strong and healthy; he let his mother know he was hungry too. Quinn pulled a warm blanket up around his new son and his wife, then went to find his other two boys. He brought them over to where Dahteste was laying.

"Boys," Quinn whispered, "meet your new little brother. His name is Little Flynn."

Quinn looked up at his wife and she nodded in agreement. The oldest boy, Connor, looked his new brother over carefully. Collin and Ragan fell back to sleep snuggled up next to their mother. Rufus had to get in on the act too, but when he found the bundle was just another little boy who would chew on his ears, too, he lost interest and laid down next to Dahteste.

"Why is he all wrinkly, papa?" the boy asked earnestly.

"That's just the way little babies look," Quinn replied. "You were too, ya know."

"Do we get to keep him too, like Collin and Ragan?" the boy asked.

"We sure do," Quinn smiled, "we sure do."

"Papa," the little boy yawned, "I'm awful tired, can I go to sleep now?"

Dahteste raised the right side of the blanket and let her oldest son climb into the makeshift bed. Before long all five of the people Quinn held most dear were asleep. Old Rufus crawled over to where Quinn was sitting.

"June 24, 1881, an hour before sunrise I reckon, Ruf. Now ya got another Duncan to look after." Quinn smiled.

He scratched the mutt behind his ears.

"Ya know, old boy," Quinn said wistfully. "If your name sake hadn't have saved my life, none of this would have been possible. S'pose he's proud looking down now? I hope so . . . Rufus, thank you."

The rest of the summer passed without much of a ta do. The work around the ranch went well. Both the horse and cow herds had grown in size and quality. With that the demand for more land became necessary. A couple of the neighbors, sodbusters, gave up and left. Each had a section of land so the Duncan boys bought them out . . . they didn't just steal the land like the yahoos over at the Bar Cross T would do. No, the Duncans gave the settlers the going rate for their land. After the deal was made and the deed signed, Quinn and Flynn discussed what to do with their new acreage.

"Ya know, brother," Flynn mused, "I wonder when these farmers are going to figure out you can't farm this high up in the foothills."

"Yeah, I know," Quinn replied. "Too bad too, the Jensons and the Hughes were nice people. I hope they have better luck in Oregon."

"Did your travels ever take you to Oregon, brother?" Flynn asked.

"No," Quinn replied, "I pretty much stayed in the Colorado and Wyoming country. Didn't hear tell of any gold strikes in Oregon. Why?"

"I been there," Flynn remarked. "Pretty country. Mostly farmers though. There were a couple of outfits in the Owyhee country and down into Nevada. So I just kept moving southeast until I got here. My compadre and I had rounded up some wild cattle and was taking them into La Cueva when we got bush whacked."

"Ya know, I been thinking don'tcha think we better start plannin' for Hank and Katie's futures?" Quinn said.

"Funny you should mention this, brother. I been thinkin' the same thing," Flynn answered.

"Yeah, one of these days some young cowpoke is gonna start sniffin' 'round here asking for Katie's hand and you better be prepared." Quinn laughed.

"Brother, what are you talkin' about, Katie's just a child," Flynn protested.

"Child hell. Have you taken a good look at her lately? She's pert near seventeen and won't be long before some young fella comes around. You can take that to the bank. Not only that, Hank is a man full grown. We made him a partner sure, but a man wants to have his own place. I think we oughta give him one of those sections so he can start his own place before he takes a notion to strike out on his own," Quinn said.

The color drained out of Flynn's face as though someone had gut punched him, then kicked him when he was down. The kids weren't his by birth, but he had raised them as his own since he and Gwenny got married thirteen years ago. He knew this time would come, but Quinn's words brought the time right up to his face and he wasn't ready.

"Damn," Flynn groaned. "I think I'm going to be sick. I guess Gwenny and I need to talk, huh?"

"I'd say so." Quinn chuckled.

About then, Dahteste appeared from the garden with three young boys trailing along and the fourth strapped to her back.

"Why does my husband laugh?" she asked.

"Oh my little brother can't see the forest for the trees."

Dahteste's quizzical look told Quinn he said something else white folks say that Indians don't understand.

"Katie and Hank have grown into young adults and he hadn't even noticed. I guess he seemed to think they would stay kids forever." Quinn laughed again and shook his head.

"Your time will come, husband," Dahteste, ever wise, observed.

Quinn was incredulous. "Me? No, uh, uh. Here let me help you with the vegetables."

"Thank you, Quinn." His wife smiled. She shook her head and walked ahead of him to the house.

"What?" he said.

Quinn's warning was downright prophetic because within the next few days a young man came callin' to ask Katie to a barn dance and social at the McGovern place the coming weekend. The young man worked for Silas and Flynn had ran into him a time or two in town getting supplies. Flynn and Hank were in the corral working a young colt. Well, Hank was working and Flynn was watching . . . Hank was the horse trainer.

"Howdy, Mr. Duncan," the young man said amiably. "I was hoping to see Miss Katie . . . if that's okay with you that is. I was wanting to invite her to the dance this Saturday, with your permission."

The young man was obviously shaking; so much so, Flynn and Hank were surprised he could stay in the saddle. Flynn jumped down off the fence and rose to his full height, which was considerable. Hank followed suit. The two men presented an intimidating pair that left the young man rethinking the wisdom of asking Katie out. For her part, Katie was watching the scene play out from the clothesline, wondering if the young man would faint dead away. Finally, Flynn spoke.

"Well, ya better climb down before ya fall down," Flynn said. "If ya want Katie to go to the dance, ya better ask her yourself. There she is."

"Yes sir," the young man stammered, "thank you, sir."

Hank couldn't help but laugh.

"I hope I wasn't this scared lookin' when I asked Betty McGovern on our first outing."

"I think you had a little more backbone," Flynn replied. "You had the advantage of workin' for Herman when he was laid up with that busted leg. He kinda likes you. By the way, when are you two gonna tie the knot. You been walkin' out together for a couple years; what are you waitin' on?"

"Ya know, pa, funny you should mention that," Hank acknowledged. "Betty and I have been talkin' about marryin'.

We just haven't settled on a time, yet. And I want to be able to provide for her better than a cow hand's pay."

Flynn was a little insulted.

"Just hold on boy," Flynn declared. "You're makin' more than cow hand's wages. Shoot, you're a partner; you own a piece of this place. As a matter of fact, Quinn and I were talkin' 'bout givin' you the section we just bought from the Jensens. Granted that ain't a lot of land, but there's room to grow. You could build a good place to raise a family."

Hank was truly shocked and grateful.

"Pa," Hank said earnestly, "I don't know what to say. Thank you, pa . . . you and Uncle Quinn both."

"Well," Flynn grinned, "we can call this a weddin' present. We'll go see Quinn and go to town and get the deed changed over to your name toot sweet."

Now that was easier than I expected, Flynn thought. He watched Hank swing up easily into the saddle. I don't imagine Katie is gonna be that easy. He looked over to the garden where Katie and Matt Griffin were talking, no sir not easy at all.

Katie thought about making the young man squirm, but she took pity on the handsome, somewhat awkward young cowboy.

"I'd be happy to go to the dance." Katie smiled coyly.

"Ya will?" Matt gushed. "Why I'll be the envy of all the other fellas there. I'll come by at six to get you, if that's alright."

"That will be fine, Matt. I'm looking forward to the dance. I'm sure my friends will be envious of me, as well." Katie beamed.

Katie bent down to pick up the laundry basket.

"Here, Miss Katie," Matt said, "let me help you carry this to the house for ya."

"Why thank you, Matt. And please, just call me Katie," the girl replied.

Flynn wondered how this would play out. Matt wasn't the first boy who came sniffin' around the place looking to get close to Katie, but none of them had the guts to run the gauntlet of Duncan men. Matt was the only one who had the courage to actually ask for a date. Flynn had to give him credit for that. Matt had showed up in the valley about five years earlier. He was just a kid down on his luck lookin' for any kind of work. Old Silas McGovern took a chance on Matt; he had a hunch the young man was a worthwhile kid and he was right. Matt rode past Flynn on his way to the main road to town.

"Good day, Mr. Duncan," Matt said.

He sat tall and proud in the saddle, brimming with confidence after his successful quest. But that all changed with just one sentence from Flynn.

"Don't be thinkin' of takin' any improper advances with my little girl, boy. I'll be there watchin'," Flynn growled.

Matt cringed noticeably.

"No sir, I wouldn't ever do that," the boy stammered.

"Just see that ya don't," Flynn added as Matt rode on.

Katie heard the exchange and was decidedly outraged and gave her father a good dressing down.

"Daddy!" Katie began, "how could you treat Matt that way. He is the nicest boy around the territory and he would never take advantage of a situation. Besides, I can take care of myself, you raised me to be independent. You're unfair and intolerant. Not only that, you embarrassed me. You owe Matt an apology."

While Katie stomped away, Flynn stood there dumbfounded. His little girl really had grown up.

Quinn had brought his family over for a visit and he and Dahteste heard Katie's tirade.

"You sure handled that well, little brother." Quinn smirked.

Katie banged into the house and up the stairs to her bedroom and slammed the door behind her . . . an obvious indication she didn't want visitors. Gwenny came out of the kitchen, wondering what storm had hit the house and who was to blame for the ruckus. Flynn had the misfortune of following Katie into the house. Gwenny put two and two together and her husband's number came up.

"Oh, Flynn, what did you do now?" Gwenny asked.

"Not now, Gwenny," Flynn said tersely and went looking for his Scotch.

Gwenny stood there flabbergasted for a moment, then started to go after her husband and give him a piece of her mind. On the way out, she ran into Quinn and Dahteste. Dahteste thought perhaps this wasn't a good time to visit, but Quinn said he'd take care of his brother. She and Gwenny should go talk to Katie.

"What in the world is going on?" Gwenny asked incredulously.

"Your husband is being himself again. Don't worry, I'll take care of Mr. Insensitive; you look after Katie." Quinn smiled. "Oh, if he comes in a little bruised up, don't be alarmed."

Dahteste gave Quinn a look only an Apache wife can.

"I swear, I won't hurt him," Quinn said reassuringly. Much, he thought to himself.

Although he loved his brother, Quinn didn't have much patience with Flynn's lack of empathy and seemingly unending ability to be oblivious to other people's feelings. Even though Flynn was a kind and caring husband and father, he tended to be a little too heavy handed where the rearing of his children were concerned... especially with Katie. He had to learn to let go and Quinn figured Flynn needed little "tenderizing" and he was the one man big and bad enough to get the job done. Quinn found his brother sucking down scotch under the parlay tree. He knew he needed to get his brother understanding the principle of empathy before he was too drunk to comprehend.

"I suppose you are gonna just sit here until you're blind, stupid drunk," Quinn observed.

Flynn glared at his older brother.

"And if I do, what makes you think my business had anything to do with you," Flynn snarled.

Uh-ho, Quinn thought. That made no sense, I might already be too late.

"I want to talk to you," Quinn said flatly, "I want you sober enough to understand. Give me that jug."

"Go to the devil!" Flynn thundered. "Unless you think you can take this jug from me, leave me to hell alone!"

Never one to back down from a challenge, Quinn waded in without thinking. Many years had passed since the two brothers had a fist fight and given that Flynn was half drunk, Quinn reckoned this would be easy. A heavy, iron packed right hand that sent him head over heels into the corral fence taught him otherwise. A curious filly came sniffin' around the large hulk who crashed into her living quarters. Once Quinn regained his senses, he scratched the young horse.

"Don't you worry, I'll be back directly to fix the fence." He smiled.

Once the parameters for the fight were established, Quinn went on the offensive. He wasn't going to give his younger, powerful brother the chance to lay another hand on him. Still, he felt the only fair thing to do would be to give his brother one final opportunity to give in and listen to reason. Flynn's answer to that was to take another pull on the jug and throw a wild right punch that missed its target by a mile.

"Flynn," Quinn cautioned, "remember, I warned you."

"Ha," Flynn laughed, "warned me about what?"

"This . . ." Okay lil brother, you asked for a thrashin'; you're going to get one.

Quinn decided drunk or not, he wasn't gonna give Flynn another chance to land a punch. Quinn came at him hard and fast using a combination of boxing, brawling, wrestling, and Apache hand to hand fighting. Flynn never knew what hit him. Even had he been sober as a judge, he wouldn't have stood a chance against Quinn's fierce onslaught. Battered, bloodied, and bruised Flynn threw in the towel.

"Quinn, Quinn, stop, stop! I give up," Flynn hollered.

Well, maybe hollered wasn't exactly the right word . . . more like gasped . . . but loud enough for Quinn to hear. And truth be told, Quinn was about done in too. A whole bunch of work was involved in defeating a man as big and powerful as his "lil" brother.

"Are you sure?" Quinn asked breathlessly. "'Cause if you ain't, we can continue this 'til yer sure."

"No, I'm sure," Flynn wheezed, "I had enough."

"Good," Quinn said, "this was harder than I thought. Yer a big man, hard headed too. Be right back."

Flynn lay underneath the parlay tree and surveyed the tore up ground that indicated a couple of bull bison had gotten into a shoving match. Quinn had walked a few yards away where he had tossed the jug. Fortunately the cork was still in tight and the bottle hadn't broken. Quinn poured some scotch onto a handkerchief and started cleaning the myriad of cuts on his brother's face. Of course, Flynn cried and moaned worse than Quinn's boys. Obviously, Flynn had never learned to be as stoic about pain as Apaches were . . . they were taught from the cradleboard not to show pain. Although Quinn had to wonder how he would be taking this doctoring had the situation been reversed.

"For God sakes, Flynn," Quinn cajoled, "you're worse than my boys. This can't be that bad."

"The hell you say," Flynn objected. "Let me batter up your face then pour some whiskey on the open wounds and see how you feel."

"Well," Quinn said, "you had this whoopin' comin'. You were . . . let me think . . . what did Katie say? Oh yeah, intolerant, and let me add intolerable. You were just plain hateful, insufferable, and detestable. What the hell were you thinkin? You have to face facts, brother; Katie is gonna get married and settle down one day, and if you don't back off, you're gonna lose her . . . just as simple as that."

"What do you know?" Flynn countered. "You're raising boys . . . boys is some different."

"Ya don't say," Quinn replied sarcastically. "You can't berate and intimidate every fella that comes courtin'. Besides, give Katie a little credit; she ain't gonna take up with just any ol' drifter that comes along."

"I s'pose yer right," Flynn acknowledged, "but I just don't want her to get hurt."

"I understand that," Quinn replied, "but you'll lose her quicker if you keep on actin' like you did today. And I'll tell you somethin' else. You better go apologize before you get Gwenny after yer hide too."

"Damn! I plumb forgot about Gwenny." Flynn swallowed audibly.

"Yeah, well," Quinn snorted, "you're fixin' to get your memory nudged. Here she comes and she looks loaded for bear. You think I gave you a beatin', ha!"

Gwenny was snortin' fire; and steam comin' out her ears. Quinn took the coward's way out.

"I gotta go; I got things to do. See ya . . . I hope." Quinn called for Rufus and took off for his place at a dead run.

Gwenny and Dahteste had gone up to Katie's room to comfort and calm her down. Dahteste was carrying little Flynn and Katie couldn't resist the urge to take the baby in her arms and rock him.

"One day you'll have babies of your own," Gwenny said. "You'll make a fine mother."

"Not if pa keeps acting like he did today," Katie lamented. "There won't be a boy within a hundred miles that will want to come anywhere near me. Between pa and Hank, I haven't got a chance of getting married."

Dahteste watched the interaction between the two before she spoke.

"With Apache daughters, father is much worse," she explained. "Young warrior must run gauntlet and bring large bride price. Your father loves you. He like Quinn; he will make things right."

Gwenny was ready to burst.

"He darn sure will make things right," Gwenny declared, then stormed out of the room.

Gwenny virtually leapt down the stairs and bounded out the front door, down the porch steps, and headed for the parlay tree at a dead run. She expected to find a drunk husband, but what she saw made her stop dead in her tracks. The visage of her husband wasn't what she expected at all and the anger she was going to bring down on Flynn's head evaporated in the hot New Mexico summer air. Flynn looked like he had a go 'round with a bull buffalo and lost. Before she could say anything her husband spoke up.

"Now don't start in on me too, Gwenny," Flynn said. "My big brother gave me a thorough thrashin' . . . which I had comin'; I don't need no more from you."

"Oh my good Lord," Gwenny gasped. "Your brother did that to you?"

"Yes sir," Flynn pronounced, "but being a doctor, he was good enough to take care of all the cuts and bruises he gave me. Pretty considerate, huh?"

"I had every intention of coming out here to give you a good piece of my mind," Gwenny admitted, "but under the circumstances, I'd say you've been punished enough. However, the worst part of all this is yet to come . . . you have to apologize to Katie . . . and to Matt; that won't be easy."

"I know," Flynn agreed. "I don't know what come over me. I shouldn't have acted that way. I'm really sorry."

Gwenny gently kissed Flynn's cheek.

"If I were you," Gwenny said, "I would say this to Katie. You're a good man Flynn Duncan; you just forget yourself every now and again."

"Guess there's no point in putting this off." Flynn sighed.

He turned toward the house and saw Katie and Dahteste come down to the porch. At the sight of the beaten, battered man, they both gasped.

"Pa," Katied cried, "did Uncle Quinn do this to you?"

"Yep." Flynn smiled. "My big brother thought he'd better teach me a good lesson for being such an ass. I can definitely tell you I've learned my lesson. I'm sorry, baby girl; will you forgive me?"

"Oh, pa, yes I do," Katie replied. "But, pa, you have to let me grow up and start making my own decisions. You taught me how to tell good folks from bad, from people who just want to take advantage of me 'cause we're well off. But Matt isn't like that, pa; he's a nice boy."

"I know that darlin'," Flynn confirmed, "I just lost my good sense."

"Well, what's done is done," Katie reassured. "We'll just move on. Besides, Matt is made of sterner stuff; he'll still take me to the dance. You didn't scare him off."

Dahteste quietly watched the interaction between father and daughter and was admittedly glad she had sons. Perhaps Quinn would be less protective of the boys. Still, she thought Quinn had overdone the punishment and was frankly a little taken aback. She intended to rectify the situation when she got home.

"Flynn good man. Quinn good man. Brothers alike. You both good fathers. My husband beat too hard, maybe," Dahteste said. "I will talk to Quinn; he will make amends."

"Dahteste," Flynn replied. "I got just what I had comin'. But sometimes when Quinn gets started he can't quit. I think he's still fightin' that damn war. He'll come around I know. And thank you."

Everyone embraced and Flynn helped Dahteste into the buggy. The boys jumped in like young deer.

"You want me to drive you home?" Flynn asked.

Dahteste deftly guided the team around to the road, coaxed the horses up to a brisk trot, and disappeared over the hill to her family's ranch. She found Quinn forking hay into feed bunks for the horses. The serious expression on his wife's face wasn't totally lost on him.

"Something tells me I'm in for a good dressin' down, Ruf ol boy," Quinn whispered.

That was exactly what he got too. Rather than use broken English, Dahteste used her native language to express her dissatisfaction of her husband's over reaction to Flynn's bad behavior. Quinn didn't even attempt to protest. He simply listened and nodded where appropriate. Somethin' told him, he'd be sleeping with Rufus tonight. Well, he thought, this certainly wasn't one of the Duncan brothers' finest hours.

THE HARVEST DANCE was a great success. All attendees laughed, sang, and danced until almost midnight; by then everyone was ready to bring the proceedings to an end. The Duncan family had reconciled; that was a good thing too because by all indications, Katie would soon be getting married. After the dance, Matt and Katie walked out together on a regular basis and every chance he got, Matt would come by to spend time with Katie. Flynn and Hank toned down their razzing of Matt. As a matter of fact, they found Matt to be a darn good hand, so good Flynn offered him a job. When Matt turned him down, he found out something more about the young man's character.

"Mr. Duncan, I sure do appreciate the offer," Matt said, "but I have to decline. Ya see Silas has been real good to me; he gave me a chance when no one else in the valley would. I s'pect I better continue to ride the brand I started with."

Flynn was pleasantly surprised not only about Matt's refusal, but also at the way he reacted. Ordinarily Flynn would be more than a little put out that someone had the nerve to disagree with him. But this time, Flynn found himself proud of the young man who might one day become his son-in-law. Flynn stuck out his hand to shake the Matt's hand.

"I understand," Flynn said. "And to tell you the truth, I was one of the people in the valley who turned his back on you. I was wrong; turns out I missed out on having a damn good hand working for me."

Matt was more than a little surprised at Flynn's reaction. He learned something this day: if ya want to earn the Duncan clan's respect, be honest, brave, and stay true to yourself.

"Thank you, Mr. Duncan." Matt beamed. "That means a whole bunch comin' from you. The Double D is the most respected outfit around here . . . well this sure 'nough means a lot."

The other branch of the Duncan family was also enjoying a modicum of success and peace. The boys were growing and the youngest of the brood, whenever he wasn't in his cradleboard, was crawling around getting into just about anything he could. The Appaloosa horses Quinn was raising were becoming hot commodities around the valley and every rancher around had at least one of the spotted breed in his string. The family made frequent visits to the Apache stronghold to visit family there. On one such visit, Quinn's Apache brothers voiced concern about the state of Indian affairs to him.

"Chief worried about white man. He fears white man take Apache land like Lakota and Cheyenne," Itz-chu said.

Quinn was aware of government reprisals on the Lakota and Cheyenne after the Custer debacle. Indians were forced onto reservations and relegated to live off handouts from the

Bureau of Indian Affairs, which was long on promise and short on follow through. The Nez Perce, Comanche, Arapaho, Kiowa, and any tribe you could name were all getting the same ill treatment. Gwenny called it down right barbaric. The Jicarilla had thus far managed to avoid having their land taken from them and were still living freely on their ancestral lands. But they could see the writing on the wall and were afraid.

"Norroso Taklishim think white soldiers come," Jlin-Litzoque interjected.

"I think there is a way to keep you on your land and keep the soldiers away," Quinn offered, "but Norroso Taklishim may not like my plan. We need to talk."

"All elders gather tomorrow," Itz-chu said, "Chief and White Bear talk then."

"Good," Quinn nodded, "but for now, I will go to bed."

Quinn found supper waiting him in the family's wickiup. The boys were sleeping peacefully and Dahteste was nursing the baby. She was quick to notice all the subtle nuances of her husband's expressions; she could tell he was worried.

"My husband should be at peace with Apache family," Dahteste whispered. "Why are you not so?"

"Your family is worried the white man will try to steal their land," Quinn replied. "I didn't want to say so, but they have every right to be afraid. The government is taking all ancestral land from all the tribes; they are disregarding treaties and just taking land. I have a plan, but I don't know if the tribe will like what I have in mind. They may think I am trying to steal their land too."

"What is your plan?" Dahteste asked.

"I want to buy their land and have the deed recorded in my name," Quinn explained. "The tribe will be able to live on their ancestral lands forever. The only difference will be the land is in my name, a white man. The government couldn't come in and force the Jicarilla off their land because technically, they don't own the land any longer. And as long as the land is in the hands of a Duncan, no one will bother the Jicarilla Apache. Do you understand? What do you think?"

"I think my husband is right." Dahteste sighed. "My people might think you try to steal land."

"Damn." Quinn was frustrated. "I don't know what to do. Should I not even bring up the subject?"

"Quinn should talk to Itz-chu and Jlin-Litzoque first. They agree, then talk to chief," Dahteste advised.

Quinn nodded thoughtfully.

"Wife, I'm glad someone in this family sees the truth . . . you are wise indeed. And I love you."

They wrapped each other in a loving embrace while Dahteste still held their youngest son. Quinn thought how could anyone hate this small little child enough to want him dead? He couldn't wrap his mind around the kind of person who would kill women, old men, and children because of the color of their skin. He had fought a war to end slavery and hatred and while the fighting may have stopped, an emancipation may have been proclaimed, but the hearts and minds of many people was still consumed by hatred. Since the beginning of this country, until the present, the foundation was built on the backs of black slaves and indigenous Native people. Manifest Destiny was another name for stealing as far as Quinn was concerned. He lay his head back and looked up into the night sky at the millions of stars shining brightly. Maybe one day things will change . . . someday . . . and he drifted off to sleep.

The next morning Quinn packed up supplies for a few days and left for his extended family's home. He couldn't help but wonder if he were doing the right thing or opening a can of worms he shouldn't. Only a matter of time would pass before whites would put the Jicarilla Apaches on a reservation and "legally" steal their land. He felt like he had to do something to help his family; this was all he could think to do. Hopefully, he had gained enough trust and respect from the Apache they would go along with his plan. Well, we'll see, he thought.

Quinn was met at the opening to the Jicarilla stronghold. Quinn could never get over how the Apache were aware of anyone coming near their territory without giving away their presence. Any intruder could be killed without knowing where the shot or arrow (that did the deed) came from.

"Our brother careless. He gave up position too easy," Itz-Chu said.

"Need to be careful. Might get shot—young brave anxious kill white man. Become man," Jlin-Litzoque added.

"You're right," Quinn acknowledged, "but I was thinking…"

His Apache brothers started to raise their objections, but Quinn waved them off with his huge hand.

" . . . I know that's no excuse, but I knew my brothers would protect me." Quinn grinned. "I am here to see Norroso Taklishim. I wish to talk to him about saving the Apache and their land."

The two Apaches looked quizzically at each other.

"Apache live on this land always. Ancestors live land when Spanish come. Always live this land," Itz-Chu declared.

"Yes, I know," Quinn allowed, "but all the tribes are losing land to the white government and put on reservations. I have a plan that may save my Apache brothers' lands. Let's go talk awhile; I'll explain."

The three men rode down the stream to a grove of juniper trees where they could talk without any interruptions. Quinn explained his proposal to his adopted brothers and when he was finished, the two men were more than a little unsure about the wisdom of Quinn's plan.

"What if White Bear dies, then who gets land?" Jlin-Litzoque asked.

"The land will stay in my family; Dahteste's sons will own the land. That means the land will be safe and so will the Apache for generations to come."

Quinn's Apache brothers looked at each other, then back to Quinn. They searched the big man's deeply lined face. The years of living and working out in the elements had left Quinn's face tanned and scarred. But they could detect no treachery . . . he was family.

"We talk to all the elders. Norroso Taklishim cannot decide alone. All people must decide," Itz-Chu said.

"This is good," Quinn replied. "I only want to help your people survive."

"We believe White Bear, our brother," Jlin-Litzoque declared.

The three men saddled up and made their way to the stronghold where Quinn would have to convince the entire tribe of his sincerity. Quinn was made welcome as always. His mother-in-law asked after her newest grandson, who was now nearly four months old, and her daughter. His father-in-law was more interested in talking about horses and cattle. Bod-away, Fire Maker, had become quite a good rancher . . . the other tribe members thought he had forgotten tribal ways. But the man was a realist . . . he could see the writing on the wall and he wanted to make sure he and his family would survive in a white man's world. He intended to make sure he retained the tribal culture as well. While Quinn visited with his in-laws, his adopted brothers went off in search of the chief and the tribal elders. Little time had passed until Quinn was summoned to talk with the elders. Also the entire tribe had gathered at the formal meeting place and they already knew why they had gathered.

"Vo 'kohe-Nan 'kohe, you come to take Apache land," Norroso Taklishim stated.

Whoa, using my Cheyenne name; this deal is going to be formal, Quinn thought.

"No, Norroso Taklishim," Quinn replied earnestly. "I come here to protect your land for all Jicarilla Apaches. For you and future generations. I don't want your land; I want to shield you from white men who want to steal your land."

Quinn explained his plan in detail and answered all the questions from tribal elders and individual tribe members. Then he went to his wickiup and waited while the tribe made their decision. He figured the wait would be long so he made himself comfortable. He stretched out on his buffalo robe and decided to take a nap. No sense in worrying and in no time, Quinn fell asleep. He awoke the next morning to the sun shining through the roof of his shelter. He felt a presence near him but he never so much as twitched. He looked dead to the world, but he was instantly ready to ward off whoever or whatever the threat might be. Itz-Chu leaned over Quinn's prone body who slowly opened his eyes.

"White Bear getting old." Itz-Chu laughed. "Take too long wake up. Been waiting long time."

"Is that so?" Quinn said sarcastically. "I heard you before you came through the door. I was ready for you."

Quinn raised the blanket and his Apache brother came within a gnat's eyelash of a loaded Colt 45.

"White Bear make good Apache." Itz-Chu smiled.

"Sure 'nough." Quinn chuckled. "I learned well from a fierce Apache warrior . . . your sister."

"Woman not fierce," Itz-Chu grunted.

"Really?" Quinn questioned. "If that's true, then how did you get those scars above your eye and under your chin?"

The warrior made a non-committal huff and motioned for Quinn to follow.

"Tribe ready answer, white brother."

Quinn followed along with the two men. He couldn't help but wonder what the future could hold for these people. He was sure, even with the best of intentions of men like himself, tribes all across the West would eventually be subjugated. The policy of Manifest Destiny had settled the country from one end to the other. The rule of thumb: assimilate or die. God help us all, he thought. Itz-Chu was introducing him to the tribal council; boy this really was a formal gathering.

"Vo 'kohe-Nan 'kohe," Norroso Taklishim began, "you come here to buy Apache land. You say you own land let Apache stay. Apache ask how man can own land. Creator made land for all people. Why white man buy and sell land? Why white man want all land? Why take more than need to live?"

Quinn wasn't sure how he would answer so his people could understand.

"Norroso Taklishim speaks the truth," Quinn allowed. "Most of the white men believe the Creator gave them the right to take everything on Mother Earth. They are greedy. You and I know that is wrong. The Creator wants all men to be the same. White men outnumber the Apache; they are like the stars in number compared to the Apache. They have more warriors and more weapons than the Apache. Soon they will come here and take the land like they did with the Sioux, the Cheyenne, the Nez Perce, the Arapaho, and all the other tribes. The Apache cannot win a war with white soldiers."

"Vo`kohe Nan`kohe not like other white men. You respect Apache traditions. Now you come. Want buy Apache land. You like other white men."

"No, I am not like other white men. I want to buy your land for you to keep. If the land is in my name, other white men will respect my ownership and leave the Apache alone."

"Why that so?" Norroso Taklishim asked.

Quinn had brought the deed to his property to show the Apache.

"This paper shows the land I own. This is called a land deed. I have registered my deed in the territorial capital and the land office in La Cueva. This paper says no one can take my land. I would put your land in my name also. No one could take this land either."

Jlin-Litzoque spoke up. "Let Apache have own paper. Record land."

"I would like to do that but the white man wouldn't recognize a land deed in the Apache's name. They would still take Apache land. My way is the only way for you to keep your land for future generations."

"I trust my white brother," Itz-Chu said. "Tribe should sell land to White Bear."

Quinn's in-laws spoke up next.

"White Bear made Dahteste his wife," Bodaway stated. "He has shown respect for daughter's family and culture. Trust White Bear. Never lie. Never take Apache land. Should sell land to White Bear."

One by one, members of the tribe spoke in favor of Quinn's plan. After all the years dealing with Indians, he was all at once struck by the Indians' faith in someone they trusted. They were no different than anyone else, no matter the color of their skin. Respect begets respect; pretty simple really. Norroso Taklishim looked Quinn squarely in the eyes. He felt like the chief was looking deeply into his soul; that made him a little uneasy.

"Vo`kohe Nan`kohe," the chief said. "Apache will sell land. White Bear understand. Betray Apache, you die. Family die also."

Well, now; that was pretty clear, Quinn thought. The Apache were nothing if they weren't direct and straightforward.

"Norroso Taklishim," Quinn vowed, "you have my promise. Your land will be held in trust for the Apache as long as one member of my family lives forevermore."

The chief stood and walked forward, indicating Quinn should stand. (The tribal elders stood as well.) He extended his hands to Quinn and he reciprocated in kind.

"We sign paper," the chief said.

"This is good. You, my Apache brothers, Flynn, and I will go to La Cueva to file the paperwork. Flynn will be a witness so no one can say the sale is not legal."

The chief nodded and the deal was done.

THE TRIP TO La Cueva would be quite an adventure. There was a huge entourage of Apaches and the Duncan family. The Apache were dressed in their finest regalia and when they arrived at the Duncan ranch, Flynn felt a little underdressed so he went upstairs to change into his "Sunday go to meetin'" duds. Every other member of the Duncan clan followed suit and before long everyone was ready to make the trip to town.

The land deal had an unexpected off shoot . . . the trip served as a very large family reunion. Bodaway and Liluye had a chance to visit with their daughter and grandchildren. Of course, they doted on the children. Bodaway was impressed that the boys were so fluent in their native language. Just this simple thing reinforced his belief Quinn would never betray the Apache.

"My son has shown great respect for Apache traditions. My grandsons know Apache ways and white man ways. They have two cultures. This is good," Bodaway pointed out.

"One day, as adults, they will take over the ranch; they are the future of this country. If they know both white and Apache ways, then maybe white men and Indians can live together in peace," Quinn declared.

"Yes," Bodaway agreed.

For two days, the families celebrated being together. Then everyone gathered their belongings and the little caravan headed for town. The Duncan clan's arrival in La Cueva drew the citizens' attention. No one had the slightest idea what the hell was going on.

"Sure as hell a bunch of gawkers in town today," Flynn observed.

"As far as I'm concerned, they can just gawk," Hank replied.

"Yes," Katie added. "There is no reason to stare. After all we're just people."

"I wish that were true," Gwenny said. "These people look at the Apache as trespassers. The Apache have invaded their territory, uninvited. Sadly, they would never be invited."

"Seems they dang sure better get used to having the Apache in town," Quinn announced. "High time people started getting along."

"My husband, you must give people time to adjust," Dahteste cautioned. "You make demands people might not be ready."

"They dang sure better get ready; that's all I have to say," Quinn retorted.

The entourage dismounted their horses and climbed down from buckboards in front of the recorder's office. Today would be the day a new course of action would be applied to the Indian question in regards to keeping their land. In order to stay on their land, they would sell the land. This may seem contrary to good sense, but Quinn and the Jicarilla could see no other alternative . . . short of being forced on to a reservation. The recorder, John Haverel, was taken aback when the Duncan clan and their in-laws entered the land office. He was darn near speechless and stuttered a greeting.

"G-g-good mo-mo-morning. What can I do for ya'll?"

Flynn was in no mood for polite conversation. He was on the prod and Haverel wasn't helping his mood.

"What do you think we want, ya damn fool? This is the land office ain't it? We want to record a deed for a large parcel of land," Flynn growled.

"Now hold on, brother," Quinn interrupted. "Let's give Mr. Haverel a minute to get his brain in gear. I don't imagine he's done business with the Jicarilla before. He needs time to adjust. Chief Norroso Taklishim will explain."

The chief stepped up to the counter with all the dignity and majesty he could muster, which was considerable. Norroso Taklishim cut quite a figure . . . he was a tall, well-built man who had aged gracefully. Even though he was quite old, his straight stature was truly remarkable.

"The Jicarilla will sell land to Vo 'kohe-Nan 'kohe. You call Quinn Duncan," the chief declared.

"This is highly irregular," the clerk said. "Do you have any official papers that say you own the land you wish to sell?"

Flynn was about ready to pull the lowly clerk over the counter and give him a good thrashin'. Quinn's strong hand on his arm and a simple shake of his head stopped Flynn. Norroso Taklishim surprised everyone, except Quinn, when he produced an official treaty made between the government and the Jicarilla (signed and in 1861 at the end of their war). The treaty laid out the boundaries of the land belonging to the Jicarilla Apache.

"The Jicarilla have treaty. White man agree to land Apache own. We sell land to Duncan."

Haverel was in total shock. There was no way he could prevent the land exchanging hands from the Apache to the most powerful family in the territory . . . and married into the Apache tribe. Finally, Quinn spoke. About damn time too, Flynn thought. Course now, Flynn wore a sarcastic smirk on his lined face.

"Mr. Haverel, I would like you to draw up deed, right and legal, naming me as the owner of the land, which will be passed down to my sons or daughters for perpetuity. No one will have any say in the disposition of the land other than my descendants and Norroso Taklishim and his descendants."

"Very well," Haverel said. "The sale and exchange of the land will be effective this day, October 25, 1881, in the township of La Cueva, New Mexico Territory."

Haverel completed the necessary paperwork and indicated where the buyer and seller should still sign their names. To everyone's surprise, the chief signed his name rather than making a mark.

"Make out two more deeds," Quinn demanded. "A stamped and notarized copy for me and one for Chief Norroso Taklishim . . . just in case yours gets misplaced if there's a fire. Can't be too careful?"

Flynn and the rest of the Duncan clan were near to bustin' happy. They could hardly contain themselves. As for Itz-Chu and the rest of the Apache delegation, they were a little more reserved, but Quinn's adopted family allowed themselves a wry smile.

Now that they had made one petty bureaucrat's day, the next stop was to the bank to do the same for the tight-fisted Orville Doner, the bank president. Quinn was sure the old scrooge had the first penny he ever made. When folks got into a financial bind and needed a loan, old man Doner was the man to come to. The only problem was, they were usually refused or charged exorbitantly high interest. Naturally, the collateral he wanted was the borrower's land. If they defaulted on the loan, they listed their land. Doner picked up a lot of land. That's where Quinn and Flynn came in; they usually loaned money to folks interest free. They could either pay or work off the loan. Sometimes the Duncans would take livestock in trade. Whatever the situation, the Duncans transactions never failed to irritate Doner no end. Flynn always said he would never do business with the bank . . . except old Orville had the biggest, heaviest, fire proof, and robber proof safe in the territory. The Jicarilla's money would be safe there. Doner nearly choked when the Duncans and the Apache entered the bank.

"Well, well," the banker gushed, "how nice to see you and your family Quinn . . ."

Quinn and Flynn glared.

" . . . uh, Mr. Duncan . . . always a pleasure to do business with you. How can I help you today?"

The man's insincerity was palpable. They always felt like they needed to take a bath when they finished a transaction with Doner.

"I want to make this short and sweet . . .no palaverin' . . . just do what I tell you,"Quinn commanded.

Orville understood immediately Quinn meant business.

"Of course," the banker blathered, "what would you like me to do?"

"I want fifty thousand dollars from my account; I want to open an account for the Jicarilla; and I want you to deposit the fifty thousand into the Apache's account. Then I want you to notarize these bills of sale."

Orville Doner had never performed a transaction of this nature in his life. Oh he had transferred large amounts of funds for the Duncans before, but never when one of the parties were Indians. This particular transaction made the Apache one of the wealthiest people in the county. Whether he liked the idea of not, there was nothing he could do but comply with Quinn's wishes. The parties signed the forms where required and left the bank. Just about everyone in town watched the group mount up, load up, and leave town. Flynn had to make a stop at the general store. Gwenny raised an eyebrow and smiled knowingly. Quinn smirked as he rode by.

"What?" Flynn said. "All this business calls for a celebration, ain't that so?"

For the first time, Hank agreed. He was finally old enough to enjoy a glass of good Scotch whiskey.

"You bet, pa. Don't ya think a drink or two would be alright, ma?"

"Yes, Hank," Gwenny agreed. "As long as you don't overindulge."

Gwenny looked past Hank and straight at Flynn, who couldn't help but get his wife's meaning.

"Of course dear." Flynn smiled.

WITH THE APACHE land arrangement complete and fall work done, the Duncans were settling in for the winter. This was a time of plenty . . . and there was a good deal of plenty. The cattle and horse operations were going full speed; the family sure didn't have to worry about money. Their children were growing; Katie and Hank were young adults . . . Katie even opened her own accounting business. That was something a woman was never allowed to do, but then Katie was a very determined young woman. Hank was taking over more and more responsibility for the day to day operation on the ranch. So much so, Flynn felt free to take Gwenny on little trip. But first, there would be a weddin' or two to attend.

Hank finally got around to asking Betty McGovern to marry him and they decided on a fall weddin' . . . November 10 . . . Matt and Katie planned on a weddin' sometime around Thanksgiving. That didn't give the families very much time to plan and get the invitations out. These events called for a family meeting.

"Beats me how you two dragged your feet for so long about getting hitched and now all of a sudden, you want to set the dates practically on top of each other. How do you expect your mother to get everything done in time?" Flynn complained.

Gwenny gave Flynn a look of disapproval.

"I didn't plan on doing all the work myself, Flynn," Gwenny admonished.

"I know, wife," Flynn agreed. "Katie will help, but still . . ."

Gwenny just shook her head.

"I think Gwenny expects a good deal of help from you, ya thick head," Quinn interjected.

"Me?" Flynn asked incredulously.

"Yes, you," Gwenny declared.

"Oh, yeah, well sure I will help," Flynn said sheepishly.

"This is family celebration. Everyone will help. You too, my husband," Dahteste added. "We don't have much time and need much help."

Quinn squirmed a little, but he was all in.

"Good. Now that we have determined there will be lots of help, just what do you ladies want done?" Quinn asked.

"I think we should ask Katie and Hank what they want. After all, this will be their day," Gwenny said. "Children, what do you want?"

Hank and Katie looked at each other.

"All of us, Matt and Betty included have been thinking we could have . . . a . . . a, you know . . ."

Hank looked helplessly at Katie.

"A double wedding," Katie explained. "That would be easier to plan in a shorter time."

"Oh that's a wonderful idea," Gwenny agreed. "We should go over to the McGovern place and visit with Betty to get her ideas too."

Dahteste had been listening and offered an idea about the time.

"Perhaps you have wedding on Thanksgiving Day," she suggested.

"I never thought of that," Katie exclaimed. "What a great idea; after all, we have so much to be thankful for, right Hank?"

"That's for sure," Hank agreed. "Thanksgiving's the date."

"Thank you, Dahteste," Katie said, "I hope you know how much we love you and are glad you are a part of our family. Plus you take good care of Uncle Quinn . . . he'd be lost without you . . . we all would. You are very wise."

"Thank you. I'm proud to be part of your family," Dahteste replied. "Shall we go see Betty?"

"Yes, let's do that," Katie agreed.

"Does Matt have anything to say about this here double weddin'?" Flynn asked.

"Of course, pa," Hank said. "Just like me; the women tell us when and where we need to be, then we're there. Simple as that."

Flynn looked at Quinn.

"What's this world comin' to, brother? The next thing ya know, women will get to vote. Where will we be then?" Flynn wondered.

Quinn looked lovingly at Dahteste.

"In a much better place, brother. A much better world than we have now," Quinn observed. "Let's crack open that Scotch whiskey and have us 'a celebrate.' C'mon, Hank; Flynn go get the jug. Ladies, have a good day. By the way, when you see Matt, send him the over."

With that, the three men sat under the parlay tree for the afternoon, proud of themselves for their contribution to the wedding planning. The ladies laughed and talked all the way to the McGovern place. They all agreed the men would be mostly underfoot and would be of little help, so upon arrival at the BarMC, they sent Matt over to drink with the other three men. Betty looked at Silas sitting at his desk and suggested he and a second bottle of Scotch accompany Matt to the Duncan ranch. With all the men out of the way, the ladies got down to the business at hand.

"Now, with the men out of the way, we can get some planning done," Gwenny observed. "The first thing is to decide where to hold the ceremony."

Katie and Betty were stunned for a moment. Both girls just took for granted the ceremony would be held at their respective homes, but a double ceremony changed that.

"That's right, mother, I never gave the location a second thought," Katie remarked.

"I didn't either," Betty acknowledged. "Do you have something in mind, Mrs. Duncan?"

"Actually, Dahteste suggested a place, right?" Gwenny said.

"Yes, there is a place. The spring between ranches. To my people, sacred place. Quinn and I married there," Dahteste replied.

"What a wonderful idea," Katie said enthusiastically, "don't you think, Betty?"

"Oh yes," Betty replied, "I heartily agree."

"Well, that was easy," Gwenny said. "The only thing that might be a problem is Thanksgiving weather . . . a chance of snow."

Everyone looked from one to the other, but once again Dahteste had a solution.

"Dig large fire pit. Men can build large tent to cover people in case of snow. This will keep all the people warm and dry. Also people wear warm winter clothes and boots. I will provide wedding dresses for Katie and Betty. This will be gift from Quinn and me."

"Dahteste, that is a great idea," Gwenny said, "and this will give the men something to do."

"Very true, Gwenny," Betty agreed. "Hank has been driving me crazy lately . . . asking about wedding plans. Now I have something to tell him."

"I know what you mean, Betty," Katie added. "Matt keeps asking if there is anything new with the planning."

"Ladies," Gwenny laughed, "at least they are taking an interest; Flynn and Quinn are happy to sit back and let the women folk do all the work. Won't they be surprised when they learn they get to dig holes and build awnings?"

All the ladies laughed. Dahteste added an interesting observation.

"Men drinking today. They should start work tomorrow. Sweat off poison in their bodies. Get rid of headaches. Teach them good lesson to stay away from whiskey."

"That's for sure. Dahteste," Katie said. "Except Hank, Matt, Pa, and Uncle Quinn would spend the day soaking in the spring instead of working."

"Katie, you will learn." Dahteste smiled. "Don't let them come in house until work is done. Too cold to sleep outside. Men have become soft. Won't like to stay out, rather be in warm bed in house. They get work done, right Gwenny?"

"Very true, Dahteste," Gwenny mused. "Don't you think we had better educate these soon to be brides about what they need to know about being good wives?"

Dahteste nodded. "Yes, very important to learn to be good wife."

So, for the rest of the afternoon, the women talked about the pitfalls of marriage and how to avoid them. Needless to say, there was a good deal of good natured jokes at their men's expense. If the drinking crew only knew what lay in store, they probably would have stopped their revelry and sobered up . . . quickly.

The time proceeding Thanksgiving and the nuptials passed quickly. Dahteste's words proved prophetic as the men spent a miserable day or two recovering from their celebration. But they had to suffer through to make their children . . . . and wives . . . happy. The pit got dug and the awning was finished with ample time to spare. Flynn and Quinn did the work for the wedding while Matt and Hank tended to the ranching operations. Gwenny and the girls worked on wedding invitations and planning the combination wedding/ Thanksgiving meal while Dahteste was busy sewing the wedding dresses. And everyone prayed there wouldn't be a November blizzard that would ruin the ceremony.

One week before Thanksgiving found Quinn and Dahteste snug and warm in their parlor. A bright fire shed a warm glow throughout the room. The boys were lying by the fire playing with Rufus; Quinn stood by the window, holding the baby and watching snow drift softly to the ground. There was a good foot of snow already on the ground and this steady snowfall would add another six inches of so.

"I'm sure glad we got all the invitations passed around before the snow came," Quinn noted.

He walked over to the rocker by the fire and sat down.

"Wonder how many Jicarilla will attend? I hope they know they are welcomed," Quinn mused.

"Husband, my people are our family and that makes them Flynn and Gwenny's family. They will come. They will bring food and gifts," Dahteste pointed out. "You and your family have always shown respect to the Apache. They will show you same respect."

Dahteste was right; just about the entire tribe was in attendance from the tiniest baby to the oldest of the elders. In addition, most of the community of La Cueva and folks from surrounding ranches came as well. The weather even cooperated: the sun came out and reflected brightly off the snow. The men had outdone themselves in preparing the area for the wedding. Besides the fire pit and awning, they had built a platform so folks could dance. People would be talking about this shindig for years to come. As for Quinn, on this Thanksgiving Day and this particular occasion, he took time to reflect. He had come full circle, from a broken lonely man to a man who had a home, a family, and friends he could count on. Yes indeed, he had so much for which to be thankful.

THE NEXT FIVE years sped by without too many difficulties. The Double D grew exponentially and, by the summer of 1886, the ranch was the largest in the territory. The combined Duncan family now included grandchildren: Katie and Matt and Hank and Betty now had children (more boys, which made Flynn happy beyond words). Silas McGovern passed on and left his twenty thousand acre ranch to Matt and Betty. Hank and his accountant wife made some very smart land deals and expanded the section Flynn and Quinn gave them to a whopping ten thousand acres. Granted this ranch was still small when compared to the Double D fifty thousand acre ranch, but they were satisfied and their parents were proud. Quinn owned another fifty thousand acres, plus seventy thousand acres he held in trust for the Jicarilla Apaches. A mathematician wasn't need to figure out a very large chunk of the territory was controlled by the Duncan boys and their families.

Quinn and Dahteste's family was growing rapidly also. Their four boys ranged between the ages of ten and five. They were all of school age now. As much as their parents wanted them to maintain their Apace culture, they both agreed the boys should be educated at the local school in La Cueva. The boys weren't crazy about the idea, especially Conner, who was beginning to display his Scottish heritage of being a bit stubborn. However, with the right amount of cajoling and reasoning, Quinn and Dahteste convinced him going to school in town was the most logical choice. In addition, Quinn put his foot down so there was no other choice. As for Conner's younger brothers, they were smart enough to stay out of the fray and obediently did what their parents asked. There was a compromise: every summer the boys would go live with their grandparents in the Jicarilla stronghold.

There had been many changes for the Jicarilla as well. For the most part, the Indians wars were over. All the tribes were living on reservations. Even Geronimo, the last of the Apache to stand against the US Calvary finally surrendered. He and his Chiricahua band surrendered to Lt. Charles Gatewood in 1886. The last of twenty-seven, including women and children, were exiled to Florida. As for the Jicarilla, the Duncan purchase of their land proved to be fortuitous because more than once did the government try to move them off "their" land. Each time, the Apache and the Duncan clan thwarted the government, because legally, the Jicarilla didn't own the land and Quinn could allow anyone he wished to live there.

Flynn would always laugh and say, " . . . does my heart good to see those sons a bitches lose."

There were sad times as well. Bodaway was killed in a hunting accident; some folks thought he was murdered by a disgruntled rancher, but nothing was ever proven. (Quinn figured the score was evened when the rancher was killed in a stampede; no one could figure out how the herd stampeded, but then no one really investigated either. The immediate parties knew the truth; that was good enough.) The unique thing about Indian culture is there is no immediate family . . . the entire tribe is family. When husband and father dies, the remaining family members are taken cared for. In this instance, Liluye moved in with Itz-Chu . . . no one was left to fend for themselves.

The Jicarilla were probably the wealthiest tribes in the country. They had large herds of cattle and horses and, what was most unusual, had money in a white man's bank. They used their wealth in enterprises that would help the tribe: they built a school (Betty was the teacher) and a hospital. They already had a doctor in the family (Quinn) who made routine calls to the Jicarilla to check on folks who were sick or injured. He delivered many Apache babies as well. Combined with white man's medicine and traditional tribal healers, the were no medical troubles for which there was no answer. All-in-all everything was going swimmingly. So why couldn't Quinn shake a feeling of impending doom?

Dahteste and Quinn were out riding, something they often did one cool autumn days. Just the two of them, no children, just husband and wife enjoying the country and the day together. Dahteste hadn't lost her keen intuition where her husband's feelings were concerned. He could hide them pretty well from most everyone except his wife.

"What troubles you husband?" Dahteste asked.

"I don't know." Quinn sighed. "I guess I can't stand prosperity. I can't shed the feeling something bad is going to happen."

"Your sleep has been uneasy. You call out my name and tell me to get down, then you wake up shaking," Dahteste whispered. "Won't you tell me what troubles you?"

"Remember when I went to see the Wisaco Sani? He sent we on the quest to find my demons and interpreted my vision, saying the war would never be over for me until I returned to where I fought the worst battle . . . Gettysburg," Quinn explained.

"You should make that journey; face your fears, Quinn," Dahteste stated.

"I would . . . except . . . that isn't all. Because in my dream, you and the boys are on the battlefield and someone, whose face I can't see is trying to kill you. I shout for you to get down, but you can't hear me over the noise of the battle. I'm pinned down by Rebel fire and can't get to my rifle. Finally, at the last moment, I reach my gun and kill the sniper; he falls dead, face down. I wake up before I can see who fired."

"Then you won't make the journey alone . . . we will all go," Dahteste declared. "And there will be no argument."

Quinn sat on his horse in stunned silence. Well, old boy, no point in arguing, he thought. I guess we'll be going on a family trip.

WITH THE CARE of the ranch left to Flynn, Quinn and his family were all packed and ready to leave. Seemed like the entire Duncan clan were at the train stop to see their relatives off. This was quite an occasion, Quinn hadn't been east of the Mississippi for twenty-three years and he swore he would never go back. But an unseen force beyond his control was pulling him back. He wasn't sure of the wisdom of this trip, but he knew he would never be at peace until he confronted whatever was the cause for his nightmares.

"For the hundredth time Quinn, everything will be fine," Flynn reiterated. "Now go do what you have to do and get back home."

Gwenny helped Little Flynn onto the train steps.

"Dahteste, are you sure you wouldn't rather leave the children with us? We'd be more than happy to look after them for you."

"No thank you, Gwenny. The children must learn about their father's past. They must see their father's world," Dahteste affirmed.

Quinn helped Dahteste up the steps of the railroad car, then turned to Flynn and Gwenny.

"Well, I guess we'll be on our way; we'll see you in about a month," Quinn said. "Take care of my interests."

"Hmm," Flynn grunted, "I love you too, brother."

The family settled in for their long journey. Although this trip would take about the third of the time Quinn spent coming out West over twenty years previously. The train, with a couple of transfers, would take them all the way to Independence, Missouri. They would get on a paddle steamer down the Missouri to the Mississippi, and then all the way up the Ohio to Pittsburgh. From Pittsburgh, they would take the train to Gettysburg, Pennsylvania.

"Papa?" Collin asked. "Why are we going to this place?"

"Have you learned about the Civil War at school?" Quinn asked.

"Yes, Papa," his son replied. "That war was between white brothers to end slavery. But I think the war was more about land and money, papa."

The young boy was very bright and perceptive.

"You could very well be right, Colin. Seems like wars are always fought for wealth and power, rarely are they fought for people's rights," Quinn admitted. "Anyway, I am coming here because this is the last battle I fought in this war. But I left here with my battle unfinished. Wiscao Sani told me I had one more battle to fight before the war would be over for me. This place holds the answers I seek."

"Does this battle involve us too?" Collin asked.

"Yes, son, I'm afraid so. The dreams that plague me also involve your mother, your brothers, and you. I've always tried to keep you from harm, but I'm afraid now, I may not be able to do so and for that I am sorry," Quinn whispered.

"Papa," the brave young man said, "we are family . . . we fight battles together. That is the way of the Apache."

Quinn looked into his son's face and saw not fear, but fierce determination. In Dahteste's eyes, he saw unabashed pride.

"Our son is more of a man than we might have thought, my husband."

"He's too young to be a man; he has a long life ahead of him," Quinn remarked. I hope, he thought.

The train sped across the prairie that were once covered with buffalo were now covered only with their bones. The once proud Plains Indians: the Sioux, Cheyenne, and Comanche were just about all rounded up onto reservations. Their ancestral lands were under the plow. Farms and towns now dotted the prairies and while the west wasn't totally dead, the West Quinn traveled into twenty some years past, was certainly in its final death throes. In another ten or fifteen years, the United States would be completely civilized: Manifest Destiny was a complete success. He looked down at his sons sleeping in his lap. He couldn't help but wonder what kind of world they would live in: they were neither white, nor Apache. His wife was Apache, but she had given up her tribal life to live in his world. How would they fare without him? He hoped he would live long enough to see them to adulthood and able to take care of themselves and that he and Dahteste would leave this world together like the old couple Liluye told him about years before. There were too many questions and not enough answers. He could only hope the answers would be found in a battlefield he walked away from over twenty years ago.

"BOYS, TIME TO wake up," Quinn said. "Look here. This is Independence, Missouri. This is where I began my trip out west a long, long time ago. We're gonna stay in a hotel and get on that paddle wheeler over there and head up the Ohio River. We're about half way to Gettysburg."

The boys rubbed their eyes and tried to focus on what stretched out before them.

"Papa," Conner exclaimed, "this has to be the biggest town in the whole world. You could put three or four La Cuevas in this place."

"That just goes to show you how much you know," Collin chided, "there are lots bigger towns than this. They call them cities; there's one: New York City that makes this place look little, don't it, Papa."

"Yes, son, but Conner is right. Independence could fit a lot of La Cuevas here," Quinn gently corrected.

"They got any food here?" Ragan asked. "I'm hungry."

"You're always hungry." His brothers laughed.

"Look after your stomach first. The first rule of survival. Ain't that right, papa," Ragan pointed out.

"That's right son," Quinn chuckled, "and ya know what, I'm hungry too. C'mon, wife, let's take our boys to a fancy sit down restaurant."

"Are you sure Quinn? I mean we . . ." Dahteste hesitated.

She was clearly uncomfortable in these strange surroundings. Uncomfortable, she was downright afraid.

"Dahteste, you are my wife. Do you trust me?" Quinn asked.

"Yes, my husband."

"Do you think I can protect you?" Quinn asked.

"Yes, my husband."

"Do you think I would put you in harm's way?" Quinn asked.

"No, my husband."

"All right then, let's go get something to eat. And if anyone looks crossways at you or the boys, they'll be wearing their teeth in their throat," Quinn warned.

The family walked down the gangplank, down the boardwalk toward the hotel. A baggage man followed behind with a cart carrying their bags. Admittedly, they did draw some attention, if not by the biracial make-up, then by their dress. Dahteste was the most striking: she was statuesque, she was tall, nearly as tall as her husband, she walked erect, and proud. She wore a buckskin waistcoat and white blouse underneath with a turquoise pin at the neck. She wore down to the ankle black, split pants, and fancy black boots. She wore her black glistening hair tied back in one long braid, her dark eyes flashed brightly. While Dahteste was striking, Quinn was imposing. He was a giant of a man: six-foot-six, two-hundred and twenty pounds, all sinew and muscle. Quinn wore a flat brimmed black hat, long black coat, black pants, and black boots. He wore a white shirt and black tie covered by a silver vest, complete with gold pocket watch and chain. On his right hip, he wore a colt revolver; on the other hip, there hung a huge bowie knife. His brown, collar-length hair was graying at the temples, as was his mustache and goatee. The boys were dressed in suit jackets, white starched shirts (which they tugged at constantly), jeans, and boots. Yes, this family was eye catching indeed. Quinn's brilliant blue eyes shone menacingly, daring anyone to confront him or his family. But, as Flynn was wont to say, "Ya can't fix stupid." There always had to be some damn fool who wanted to spoil everyone's day.

Sure enough, some low life wharf rat (and his gang of thugs) had to open his big mouth.

"Well, lookie what we got here, boys," the man slurred. "We got us a real life injun squ . . ."

However, before he could finish the word, the man found himself slammed against the wall, with a huge bowie knife at his throat, where a tiny drop of blood oozed. The other men found their attempt to save their comrade thwarted by a Colt .45 pointing menacingly in their faces.

"Mister, I swear by all that's holy, I will cut you belly to brisket and blow that scum, you call friends, straight to hell, if you don't apologize to my wife, quick," Quinn growled.

"Sh-sh-shoot, mister, we didn't mean no harm," the man stammered.

"The hell you say! You intended to beat the hell outta me, leave me for dead, and rape my wife. You sons-a-bitches; I oughta kill you where you stand! This woman is a princess of the Jicarilla Apache; she can trace her bloodlines back thousands of years. My brothers and I came from good Scottish stock who worked hard all their lives, my brothers died fighting a war to save this union, and my sons are heirs to a two hundred thousand acre ranch. You probably don't know the name of the bastard that sired your sorry hide. Now apologize!" Quinn shouted.

This little altercation drew a crowd, but no one said a word.

"I'm getting tired of this, my wife is waiting, and my sons are hungry. Get to it," Quinn snarled.

"I-I-I apologize, ma'am . . ."

"Her name is Mrs. Duncan. My name is Quinn Duncan; these are my sons: Colin, Conner, Ragan, and Little Flynn."

" . . . Mrs. Duncan. I apologize to your boys, too."

"Now, git," Quinn ordered.

As they were fleeing, Quinn fired six shots in rapid succession at their heels to encourage them to hurry on their way. While Quinn was reloading his gun, a policeman arrived on the scene. With more than a little trepidation, the man approached Quinn.

"Sir, did you fire those shots?"

Quinn looked up and out from under the brim of his hat.

"Yes, sir, I did indeed. Do 'er again too, if someone disrespects my wife and sons."

"In that case, I'm afraid I'm going to have to ask you for your gun," the policeman said.

"What is your name, sheriff?" Quinn asked.

"Officer Grimes," the man said.

"Well, Officer Grimes, I'll tell ya what. You can ask . . ." Quinn said quietly.

Dahteste smiled knowingly and shook her head at her husband.

"What . . ."

Quinn was oblivious.

"You and your brother are so very much alike," Dahteste said. "Shall we go?"

Quinn turned and followed his family down the street, leaving the sweating policeman standing on the sidewalk. Then he turned to the baggage man.

"You married?" Quinn asked.

"Yes, suh, I is," the man answered.

"Then you understand, right?" Quinn asked.

"No, suh, no man alive understands a woman." The man laughed.

"What's your name?" Quinn asked.

"They calls me Rufus, but that was my slave name," he replied. "They call me John Martin now."

Quinn stopped short and turned to face the man directly.

"I knew a man named Rufus. He was the bravest, most selfless soul I ever met. He gave up his life to save mine during the war," Quinn explained. "John Martin, you keep that slave name and be proud of who you are. You be proud you lived through a living hell without losing your humanity. You tell your sons and their sons because we must never forget. Do you understand me, Rufus?"

"Yes, suh, I's do."

"Good."

They had arrived at the hotel and Rufus helped carry the family's bags to their room. Quinn gave the man a shiny, new twenty dollar gold piece. The man's eyes got big as half dollars.

"Rufus, you buy your wife and kids something nice with that money. Don't you ever forget to be proud of who you are or I'll have to come back here and remind you." Quinn smiled and extended his hand to Rufus. Quinn turned and softly closed the door behind the man.

The next morning, bright and early, the Duncans checked out of the hotel and waited for another baggage man to take their luggage to the boat. Low and behold, when Quinn turned toward the door, there was Rufus waiting patiently.

"I's here to take y'all to the steamboat, suh," Rufus announced. "Can't leave this to no one else, suh."

"Thank you, Rufus, we appreciate that," Quinn replied.

While they walked to the boat, Quinn asked what the boys thought of staying in a hotel and eating in a fancy restaurant.

"So, now that you boys have had a taste of city life, am I gonna be able to keep you on the ranch? What did ya think about the hotel?"

"Okay, I guess, papa," Collin replied. "The bed wasn't much different than mine at home, but . . ."

"At least at home I don't have to share my bed with Collin," Ragan complained. "Conner hogs the covers and Collin snores."

"I do not snore!" Collin shouted.

"You do so!" both Ragan and Conner agreed.

"Boys," Dahteste said sharply, "You need not argue. Your father has taught you better."

"I did ask, ya know," Quinn pointed out, "and I've taught the boys to be honest, right. My pa used to say, 'If ye are afraid of the answer, dinnae ask the question.' and he was right. I guess we'll just have to let you sleep on the floor when we board the boat."

That brought the boys up short. In unison, they responded. "No, papa. Any bed will be fine."

"I'm almost afraid to ask, but how did you like your meal in the restaurant?"

"Really good, papa, really good," the boys responded.

Dahteste smiled appreciatively at Quinn, knowing full well his parenting style usually got the intended results.

"How 'bout you, wife?" Quinn inquired. "You got anything to say?"

To Ragan she responded. "Your father snores more loudly than bull buffalo." Dahteste winked.

"I beg to differ." Quinn was obviously insulted. "I do not sound like a bull buffalo."

"Yes you do!" everyone responded.

End of discussion.

THE FAMILY BOARDED the paddle wheeler and began the river trip that would eventually end in Pittsburgh, some fifteen hundred miles to the east. The trip would take some ten days to two weeks, whereas in the days of the pioneers, the trip took three months. [ed. note: today we could make this trip in a matter of hours.] He couldn't help but think back to the first trip he made down this river. He was running away from the bloody conflict raging in the east. But more than that he was running from himself. Today he was a whole happy man with a family, a home; he was a prosperous man who was highly respected in his community. Still, he was a haunted man and if Wisaco Sani was right, this trip was the only way to end the haunting nightmares. The boys were really impressed at the size of the stateroom they'd share.

"Papa," they shouted in unison, "is this room all for us?"

"Yes, boys, your room is connected to ours through this door," Quinn explained. "You can come and go from your room to ours. Now you listen, 'cause this is very important. Under no circumstances are you to go out through your outside door to the main deck. You keep that door locked at all times, from the inside. Do you understand?"

The boys could see their father was deadly serious. They all nodded as Quinn continued.

"You boys don't go outside without your mother or me with you, okay? Collin, you're the oldest so I expect you to look after your brothers. Boys, you pay attention to Collin and Collin don't take advantage of your position as the oldest. Remember, you are Apache. Be proud, but not cocky. Now that that's settled, let's go see what this boat has to offer. Wife, give me your arm and we'll go."

Dahteste tucked her arm around Quinn's and they walked down the main promenade. They were a striking family; they could have been royalty. In actuality Dahteste was royalty and she walked with the grace, the stature, and self-assurance of one who was proud of who and what she was. Quinn was proud that he was the man who Dahteste had chosen to spend her life with. The boys walked before them as proud of themselves as they were their parents. People who came in contact with them were impressed and the men nodded or tipped their hats; the women nodded and curtsied. The boys lost their aplomb when they saw the paddle wheel churning water that propelled the steamboat up the river.

"Papa, Mother, look," Ragan called. "How does this wheel work?"

"Well, the steamship is run by heating water (with coal) to create steam in a boiler, similar to a train locomotive. The paddle wheel propels the boat forward. The steam and the wheel work together to make the boat go forward."

Quinn pointed to the smokestack with a stream of white smoke billowing upward into the bright blue sky. About that time, the captain strolled over to where the family was standing.

"Hou ar ye," the man said in a thick Scottish brogue. "A'm Captain Angus McHenry. A'm extending m' haun to ye."

"Good afternoon, Captain," Quinn replied. "I'm Quinn Duncan. This is my wife Dahteste and my sons: Colin, Conner, Ragan, and Little Flynn."

"Ah heard of ye," the captain said. "Ye have quite a reputation."

"I'm not sure if that's good or bad, Captain McHenry," Quinn offered. "I just try to get along, my family and me."

"Ye goin' all up the way up river?" McHenry asked.

"Yes," Quinn replied, "all the way to Pittsburgh."

"Perhaps your young lads would like to go up to the wheel house and steer the boat," McHenry offered.

Quinn looked the captain over warily. For some reason, McHenry made him uneasy, but Quinn couldn't quite put his finger on the reason. Of course, the boys were all ready to go.

"We'll see, boys," Quinn said noncommittally.

The family walked down the promenade the way they came. A little way, out of earshot, Quinn and Dahteste sat down on a bench; the boys stood by the rail watching other paddle wheelers, people on the shore, and workman on their boat. Quinn stroked his mustache thoughtfully. Dahteste, who was also thinking, studied her husband's countenance carefully.

"My husband, you are troubled."

"Yeah, there's something that just doesn't add up with the friendly captain. I sure as hell don't trust him. Let's make sure we keep a close eye on the boys," Quinn cautioned.

"I agree, Quinn," Dahteste replied. "I can't see the man's soul through his eyes. This is bad."

Quinn had been watching the captain in quiet conversation with a deckhand. He was obviously giving orders that he didn't want anyone else to hear. As a protective father, he called the boys to him.

"Listen to me all of you. Under no circumstances are you to leave our cabins without one or both of us with you," Quinn commanded. "I don't trust Captain McHenry or his deck hands. I think they would take you from us, if they had the chance. They'd sell you down the river and make you work . . ."

"You mean like they did to the black men like John Rufus?" Colin asked.

"Yes, son. But also women and children. They split families apart; all for money," Quinn replied angrily. "But don't worry; your mother and I will protect you."

The family had a restful afternoon on the promenade and then adjourned to the dining room to have dinner. The family came to their room, when Quinn halted by the door. He was obviously thinking about something.

"Dahteste wait a minute. I'll be right back."

When Quinn emerged from their stateroom, he was armed to the teeth. In addition, he gave Dahteste her revolver, in its shoulder holster, as well as her knife, which she concealed on her belt, under her jacket. Neither of the weapons were visible to a passerby, but Quinn's were. He wanted to make an impression on the passengers and crew that he was no one to mess with.

Dahteste raised an eyebrow at her husband.

"Is this not a bit showy, as Flynn would say, my husband?"

"Yes sir," Quinn replied. "I just want people to know I will not be trifled with where you and the boys are concerned. Any one wants to harm you, they have me to deal with. And if something happens to me, you will have to protect yourself and the boys."

Dahteste smiled knowingly and slipped her arm in Quinn's and the family continued to the dining room. They were greeted at the door by the maitre'd.

"Sir, I'm afraid we can't allow any firearms in the dining room. You may of course, leave them here with me."

Quinn simply scowled at the poor man; end of discussion.

"Of course we can make allowances in your case. Please follow me to your table. A waiter will be with you right away," the man said. Only too happy to be away from this huge, menacing man.

Once seated, Quinn surveyed the room. Their table was on the far side; with a wall behind his back, he could see all the entrances and exits to the dining room. He could also see Captain McHenry and the first mate watching the family's every move. The sooner they got to Pittsburgh the better, Quinn thought. The old captain must have noticed Quinn was aware of his unwanted attention and so he made his way through the crowded room to their table.

"Guid eenin," Captain McHenry said cordially. "D'ya like ye're stay aboard ma vessel."

"Certainly," Quinn replied, "the boys especially are enjoying themselves."

"Ah, a imagine so. The wee lads not havin' been off the reservation," the Captain surmised . . . incorrectly.

Dahteste recognized the condescension for what it was.

"Captain McHenry, our sons do not live on a reservation, nor do the Jicarilla. My people live on their own land the Creator gave them. We live on the DD that comprises two hundred and twenty thousand acres; our sons have been educated in the white man's school as well as their Native culture. They speak five languages fluently: Jicarilla, Spanish, French, German, and English. Our sons have not been deprived as you intimate."

Quinn was near to bursting with pride. His wife was not only beautiful, but also intelligent, passionate, and someone to be reckoned with in a fight.

"Captain," Quinn said curtly, "I'm sure you have many social duties to perform. Please don't let us keep you from them."

"Ay, guid nicht, then," McHenry replied, then excused himself.

McHenry slinked off to mingle among the passengers, then whispered something to the first mate who then left abruptly. Dahteste was aware of the comings and goings of the captain's crew as well as Quinn.

"We will arrive in Pittsburgh tomorrow morning, my husband. We will watch tonight. All will be well."

"If they're going to try something, tonight will be their last chance . . . and if they do try something tonight, tonight will be the night they die," Quinn growled menacingly.

BACK IN THEIR staterooms, Quinn had the boys get into the closet in their room out of the line of fire. Dahteste was sitting in the darkened corner of their stateroom, Quinn was in a similar corner in the boys' room. The parents were heavily armed with Winchesters, Colt 45s, Bowie knives, and Dahteste had her bow . . . as insurance. As a last ditch effort, Colin was armed with a Colt 45. The younger boys had knives. Dahteste painted her face for war as did her sons. Whatever was to come, they would be ready.

Dahteste had fallen asleep, but a soft touch on her shoulder brought her wide awake. In the dark, she could sense a huge figure standing over her; by the scent, she knew she had nothing to fear. Quinn stood over her with his finger against his lips indicating she should stay quiet. He pointed to the doors of both staterooms. They were about to have unwanted visitors. Let them come, Dahteste thought; they will learn what happens to evil cowards who attack in the dark to steal innocent children. They will learn, firsthand, about Apache justice.

Quinn settled quietly back in the chair in the dark corner; Dahteste was similarly seated in her room. Instantly, both doors slammed open and the air was filled with the acrid smell of smoke from blazing gunfire. The thunderous noise would have given the listener an idea a major battle was taking place . . . and they would have been right. Except this was not a battle for land or riches, but rather a battle to protect the lives of family. When the smoke cleared, bodies and blood were splattered over walls, doors, and decks; the intruders never knew what hit them. The Duncan family emerged unscathed, while the intruders were all dead. Quinn and Dahteste emptied their guns into the six men who tried to attack them; their bullets never missed their mark. On the other hand, the would-be murderers' shots never came close to their targets. Among the dead were members of Captain McHenry's crew: the first mate, several deck hands, and two failed gun hands. The man behind this attack wasn't present, but Quinn vowed he would soon join the men he sent to commit murder and kidnap children. Quinn reloaded his Colt 45 as he exploded out the door. He ran into another deck hand, grabbed him, and slammed him forcefully against the wall.

"Where is McHenry," Quinn raged. "Tell me or by all that's holy I will split you belly to brisket and peel your hide."

"He-he-he's barricaded himself in his room," the horrified man stammered. "He has a hostage. He says he'll kill her if you don't let him run."

"The cowardly bastard," Quinn mumbled, "we'll see."

Quinn stealthily walked along the promenade and climbed the steps to the captain's quarters. At the end of the corridor, Quinn changed his tactics. He decided, what the hell, let the bastard know who's coming for him. With every slow, pronounced step, Quinn let the jingle bobs on his spurs ring.

As though he were the grim reaper himself, Quinn slowly, methodically walked the corridor bringing McHenry's fate to him. For McHenry, the wait seemed interminable; he was nearly drowning in his own sweat. His hostage, a young girl traveling to meet her fiancé, was as frightened as a newborn fawn hiding from a mountain lion. When Quinn was within earshot, he spoke lowly, menacingly.

"McHenry," Quinn snarled, "you have no options; you are trapped like a wharf rat. There is no escaping for you; no one is coming to your rescue . . . they're dead. Come out and bring the girl with you. Either that or I'll kill you stone dead."

"I swear I'll kill this girl if you don't get me transportation out of here and a two day head start," McHenry shouted.

The captain's heavy Scots accent suddenly disappeared. Interesting Quinn thought.

"Go ahead, Captain McHenry . . . if that's your real name," Quinn challenged, "but if you do, and there is no way out of that room, I will come in after you. I promise you. You will die a slow, agonizingly painful death . . . one the Apache taught me. You will be begging me to kill you, but not before you tell me everything I want to know. The clock is ticking and my patience is wearing thin."

Silence filled an empty space. Eventually, McHenry saw the futility of his situation.

"Alright," he hollered, "I'm sending the girl out."

The door squeaked open and the frightened young woman staggered out. Dahteste immediately ran to her, wrapped her in a warm blanket, and sat down with her on a bench. The poor thing was inconsolable . . . sobbing and shaking uncontrollably; Dahteste rocked the young lady in her arms and chanted in her language . . . an Apache lullaby of sorts. Thanks to the Apache woman, the girl was able to stop crying and take a few sips of water. There happened to be a doctor aboard the paddle wheeler who took charge of the girl. By this time, Quinn opened the door wider. He stood behind the door so he could see inside through the door's crack.

"Throw out your weapons and mind you, you so much as twitch wrong and I will send you straight to hell," Quinn warned.

Immediately, a Colt and bowie knife were tossed out the door clattering onto the deck. Shortly there-after, McHenry slunk out. Quinn snatched him up by the throat and hurled him against the wall. The captain's head made contact with the wall with a loud thwack that sent him crumbling to the floor. The man lay there groveling at Quinn's feet slobbering for mercy like a rabid dog. Quinn hoisted him up once again by the throat, leaving McHenry sputtering and slavering for air.

"Quinn, stop; you're killing him," Dahteste shouted. "Dead he cannot tell us what we want to know."

Reluctantly, Quinn loosened his grip on the whining man's throat.

"You heard her. Who are you, who put you up to this, and why?" Quinn demanded, while at the same time pulling out his bowie knife.

"My name's Hollister, Zig Hollister," the man began. "I met a man in Hamilton, Ohio who said he'd pay me five thousand dollars if I kidnapped your boys and bring them to him in Pittsburgh. He wanted them alive and neither the boys, you, or your wife weren't to be harmed. I was to bring the children to Gettysburg Cemetery."

At the mention of Hamilton, Quinn's heart sank. But at the mention of Gettysburg, Quinn's blood went cold. He again tightened his hold on Hollister's throat.

"A name, Hollister, give me a name or I swear I will start carving," Quinn thundered.

Hollister grasped at the huge hands at this throat to no avail.

"Ra--gg—an . . ."

Before he could finish, Quinn rumbled, "Who did you say?"

"Ragan Duncan," Zig choked.

"You lying worthless son of a bitch," Quinn shouted. "My brother was killed at Chancellorsville."

Two thunderous fists began bashing and pummeling the unfortunate man's face until there was nothing but a bloody pulp. He raised Hollister to his feet again and asked once again who set him on their trail.

"I—I—I'm not lying," Hollister cried. "He said he spent three years in Andersonville Prison with his brother Connor; he died there. He wanted to avenge himself on you because he said you deserted and got rich. He said you had the life he should have had. I tell you, the man is crazy and he hates you more than anything."

Quinn took one hand from around the man's throat and with the other thrust his bowie knife up to the hilt in the man's guts. The man sagged to the floor, dead.

"No one hurts my family and lives," Quinn breathed.

THE TRAIN RIDE from Pittsburgh to Gettysburg was a relatively short one . . . 185 miles . . . more or less and would mean an overnight train ride. The rest of the family would sleep peacefully, but for Quinn there would be no peaceful sleep. Trying to process what Hollister told him was not letting him rest. Surely he must be lying, still a man about to meet his maker isn't about to lie. Of course, he didn't know he was about to meet his maker. Quinn left a helluva mess on the paddle wheeler—left being the operative word. He instructed the local authorities to clean up the mess and no one argued; there were plenty of witnesses who knew what happened— Quinn was only protecting his family and a young innocent girl. The big man took his family to the train station. Now, here he was trying to make sense of everything that happened the night previous. In the darkness, he felt a soft touch on his arm.

"Quinn," Dahteste's gentle voice said, "you must try to sleep."

"There is simply no way I can sleep, wife," Quinn replied.

"Not true, my husband."

Dahteste reached into her medicine bag and withdrew a small quantity of peyote.

"Here," she offered the plant leaves to her husband. "Chew this," she insisted.

"You gonna get me drunk, woman?"

"Here," Dahteste persisted.

Quinn gave in to the inevitable and took the leaves.

"Yuck," Quinn protested. "Don't you have some sugar or something to make this go down easier?"

"Stop complaining," his wife smiled, "you are not one of the boys. Relax your mind."

Dahteste hummed an enchanting Apache lullaby and massaged Quinn's temples . . . instantly, he was asleep. Dahteste smiled. Works every time, she thought. No matter how old, they are still children. She leaned against his shoulder and fell asleep as well. The next morning the family was awakened to the sound of a train whistle signaling they had reached their destination and Quinn's appointment with the past. He instructed the baggage man to see to their bags while he set off to hire a buggy; the livery stable was just across the way.

"Dahteste, you wait here with the boys, I'll be right back," Quinn stated. "Don't be afraid to use that."

Quinn pointed to the shoulder holster she concealed under her jacket.

"I won't," she replied.

Dahteste watched Quinn disappear into the livery stable and before long returned with a fine Morgan gelding drawing a beautiful, handcrafted buggy. She raised her eyebrows in approval.

"Very fancy."

"Nothing too good for my family." Quinn smiled. "You ready?"

"Wherever you lead, my husband."

"I might just lead us to our graves," Quinn said softly.

"Then we all die together, husband."

"Yes, papa," Colin added. "It is a good day to die."

"Let's hope this day isn't our last. But if that is our destiny, I want you all to know you are my pride, my strength, and I love you all with everything I have in me. Gid' up."

The ride from town to the cemetery wasn't a long one. In the intervening thirteen years since the battle, Gettysburg and the surrounding countryside had been repaired to the point, the cemetery notwithstanding, one would never know over the course of three days, 57,000 people died here. Quinn never planned to return here and as he approached the battleground his throat constricted and his pulse raced; he felt a sense of panic overwhelm him. But for Dahteste's gentle, but firm hand, he would have wheeled the buggy around and raced back to town. Slow down, he thought; breathe deeply: I wish I had some of that damn peyote now, he thought.

Quinn brought the buggy to a stop at the hill where he had been pinned down all those years ago. He reflected on his life over those years: where he'd gone, what he had accomplished, what he had to be thankful for, and what had brought him back to this place. Wicaso Sani's words returned: "You will always fight this war until you return to face the ghosts of your past. You must end this war where the war began."

At that very moment, a sense of dead calm engulfed him. He was no longer panicked; he was no longer fearful. He was a cornered mountain cat, dangerous and cunning. He welcomed the fight. He attached the ground tie weight to the horse's bridle. He gave the horse a scratch.

"Be thankful you weren't alive twenty-three years ago, fella. But today, I think you are gonna see a helluva fight."

He walked back to the buggy where his family awaited him. Like a true Apache tactician, he instructed Dahteste where he wanted she and their boys to make a stand.

"If anything happens to me, I want you there."

Quinn pointed to a prominent hill where the entire valley was in view.

"Kill anything that moves."

He embraced his boys and his wife one last time.

"We will make you proud, papa," Colin announced.

"I already am," Quinn replied.

Quinn stripped off his jacket and shirt; he pulled off his dungarees and put on deerskin pants. He slung a Winchester rifle with cartridges over his shoulder. Around his waist he wore a Bowie knife and his Colt 45 revolver. Around his head, he wrapped a blue cloth sash, on his face he wore brilliant red and blue war paint; he was ready. He let out a blood curdling war cry.

"I am Vo`kohe Nan`kohe, White Bear; I am Cheyenne; I am a warrior. Come meet me in battle, if you dare. I sing my death song; this is a good day to die."

From far off on the hill came the wailing of Dahteste's death song; her sons joined the song. If that didn't scare the hell out of everyone around for miles, they were already dead. Although truth be told, perhaps Ragan was already dead. A deathly silence encompassed the entire cemetery and surrounding battlefield . . . possibly appropriate given the circumstances.

"Well, well, well . . . if this isn't my baby brother, a coward turned savage . . ."

Ragan was the middle brother, no more than three years older than Quinn. But at fifty-one Ragan appeared much older. Obviously, the war, the internment in Andersonville, and the past twenty-one years since the end of the war spent in venomous hate had aged him fifteen years or more. The city clothes he wore seemed ill-fitting and incongruous with the man wearing them.

" . . . and over there, on the hill, must be the Apache squaw and the half-breed brats you call your family," Ragan sneered.

Quinn studied his adversary, not as a brother, but a hate-filled maniac who would stop at nothing to kill him and his family. He knew there was no reaching whatever family bond that ever existed . . . he wouldn't even try. Instead, Quinn was ready to do battle with all the skills and cunning he had been taught by the Cheyenne and the Apache. Either Quinn would die or Ragan would die; their battle was as simply barbaric as that.

"Your hate and misery have blinded you to the truth. For what happened to you, I am sorry, but there is no reconciling between us. So let us do battle and the Creator will determine the truth," Quinn said flatly.

Ragan drew his gun, but Quinn was way ahead of him. He jumped out of the way while Ragan's hand was going for his gun. Quinn's cat-like reflexes enabled him to leap onto Ragan instantly, and he proceeded to beat the ever living hell out of his older brother. Huge fists rained down on Ragan like lightning from above. Quinn was the avenging angel punishing Ragan for the harm he brought down on Quinn's family and for what he intended to bring to them. Wicaso Sani would be proud that Quinn finished his war. When Quinn was out of breath, which took some doing, he stopped.

"I should kill you for what you did to my family, but I won't, this time. But, if you ever come near my family again or send someone to harm them, I will hunt you down to hell's gates and kill you . . . Apache style . . . before I'm through you will be begging for death," Quinn promised.

Quinn had walked away when a shot rang out, a bullet grazed his head. Although a minor wound the bullet dropped him to the ground and left him dazed. One would have thought with the beating he'd gotten, Ragan wouldn't have been able to move. Still in all, he was a Duncan and the time in Andersonville had made him tough. Ragan staggered to his feet and leveled his gun at Dahteste and the boys. He could have killed Quinn, but he wanted him to live with a greater pain . . . the loss of his family. Ragan had made a calculated choice and failed. He heard Quinn's voice, but too late to save himself.

"Dahteste!" Quinn shouted. "Get down!"

A single shot rang out and Ragan fell at Dahteste's feet. Quinn had lunged for his rifle and put a bullet in the back of Ragan's head. In his nightmares, Quinn had never seen the face of his attacker; now he knew. He got up and walked to where Ragan fell. He kicked him over with the toe of his boot. At last he saw the face of his tormentor; at last his quest was finished; his war was over. Quinn picked up his brother's body, carried ot to the buggy, and laid him in the back. Oh, Ragan, find peace my brother, Quinn thought. Then, reverently, he covered Ragan's body with a blanket.

QUINN DROVE INTO town to arrange for a casket in which to transport Ragan's body home to Ohio. The local authorities didn't question Quinn's telling of the events at the Gettysburg cemetery. Seems Ragan had spent the last ten days making himself well known around town. He had been arrested for assaulting a young woman, he was involved in a shootout with a gambler, and was wanted for questioning in the death of the aforementioned young woman. All-in-all he was a man just asking to be killed.

Irregardless, he was Quinn's brother and he would make sure he was buried properly on the same farm on which he was born. Still, Quinn hated himself for killing his brother, but he knew he would have hated himself all the more had he allowed Ragan to harm his family.

Quinn arranged train tickets for himself and his family as well as space in the baggage car for Ragan's coffin. Quinn found a Civil War era American flag and covered the coffin. He nearly came to blows with the baggage handlers after they nearly dropped the coffin.

"Jeez man, watch where you're puttin' you big feet. I nearly dropped my end," the man whined.

"Quit your bellyaching. What's the difference if we drop this thing? The stiff's dead ain't he; don't make no difference to him," the man's partner explained.

Once the coffin was secured, he grabbed the offending man.

"Makes a difference to me," Quinn warned. "The man in that casket is a Civil War hero and he should be treated with the utmost respect. And what's more, he's my brother. You drop him and I'll shoot you both dead right where you stand."

Upon realizing their lives were in danger, the man apologized profusely and took better care not to repeat their mistreatment of the dead. Once aboard the train, they settled in for their overnight trip to Pittsburgh. The boys had by now become seasoned travelers, although they all admitted they still preferred horses, Quinn agreed, but this trip would have taken months horseback. Quinn looked down at his sleeping boys and wondered. He didn't know if they had been traumatized by the events on the steamship and in the cemetery. If they had been, so far there were no signs; he supposed that would take years. He hoped they understood violence was a last resort to protect their family, friends, and themselves. When they got home, he would take them to their special place. They would have a ritual sweat and he would explain their family history . . . he hoped that would suffice. By morning, the family reached the Ohio River and faced another steamship ride. This would be the easy part of the journey; the hard part would begin when they reached the old farmstead and having to face his parents. Quinn had no idea how they would react; he even thought about bypassing Ohio altogether and burying Ragan in New Mexico, but then that would be the coward's way out.

Once the steamship docked, Quinn went about securing a wagon to carry Ragan home, while Dahteste took care of the boys and seeing their belongings were taken off the boat. Quinn arrived with a buckboard and set to overseeing the care and handling of his brother. When everything was done to his satisfaction, the family headed northwest to the family farm about ten miles from town. The horses were a lively team and the ten mile trip, spent mostly in silence, took only a few hours . . . by noon Quinn turned the buckboard down the lane to the Duncan farm. The farmhouse was about a quarter mile from the main road. About halfway there, Quinn spied two men working on a fence . . . one was white, the other black. Frank and Big John had worked for the Duncan family since Quinn was a small boy. The twenty years since Quinn left and the hard work had obviously taken a toll on the two men. Quinn pulled the team to a halt and shook the men's hands. He introduced his family to the pair and followed Big John's gaze to the casket in the wagon.

"That's Mr. Ragan, ain't it?" John asked.

Actually, this sounded more like a statement than a question.

"Yes, John, that's Mr. Ragan," Quinn responded, quietly.

"How'd he die?" Frank asked.

"I shot him," Quinn said flatly.

The men should have been shocked, but they weren't.

"I had to make a choice between Ragan and my family. I'm sorry, but the choice was not difficult to make. I will allow no one to harm my family," Quinn said fervently.

"This will go hard on them," Frank remarked as he jerked his head toward the farmhouse.

"Yeah," Big John added, "but he was lookin' to get hisself killed since he came home from the war. I think he wanted you to kill him, Mr. Quinn, so's you'd have to live with his death for the rest of your born days. Kinda like revenge 'cause you didn't suffer like him and Mr. Conner done."

Quinn shook his head dejectedly.

"Yeah, well, you could be right, Big John. You two jump in the back and will go up to the house."

"Ifin' it's all the same to you, Mr. Quinn, I just as soon walk," Big John whispered.

"For God's sake," Frank chided. "The man's dead, ain't nothing gonna hurt you . . . you superstitious old fool."

Reluctantly Big John crawled into the back of the wagon while Frank jumped in behind him. Quinn stirred up the two geldings who trotted up the lane and came to a halt in front of Quinn's old home. Quinn looked the homestead over and thought wistfully how nothing had changed in the intervening years between now and the time he'd been gone. Surprisingly the house had been well kept up and Molly Duncan had brightened the front yard with a variety of colors of roses, pansies, tulips, etc. She did have a green thumb. The house had been whitewashed every few years when Quinn was a boy; to his way of thinking, not much had changed. From inside the house, Quinn could hear his mother call to his father.

"Colin, come here; looks like we have visitors."

Quinn helped Dahteste down from the wagon, while the boys scampered from the back seat to the ground. The screen door opened and Quinn's parents appeared on the front porch. Quinn hurriedly removed his hat and slicked down his hair with his hand. Dahteste couldn't help but smile at Quinn's boyish behavior.

"My God, Quinn is that you?" Molly half-whispered.

"Yes, ma'am," Quinn stammered.

Dahteste was in shock. For the first time, in the twenty-five years she'd known Quinn, this was the first time she'd ever seen Quinn intimidated by another human being. Quinn stepped forward, bent down, and allowed his mother to kiss his cheek, then he took her in his arms and gave her a long sweet embrace. Reluctantly, his mother let him go so he could shake his father's hand.

"Took you long enough to come home," his father said sternly.

"Yes sir, pa, it has been a long time," Quinn replied.

"Who's this with you? Aren't you going to introduce them to your mother and me or have you forgotten all your manners?" Colin said sternly.

"Oh, of course. Ma, pa," Quinn said proudly, "this is my family . . . my wife Dahteste and our sons: Colin, Conner, Ragan, and Lil Flynn.

The elder Duncan looked Dahteste and her boys over scrupulously. Then turned to Quinn. "Your wife is an Indian and these nits are . . ."

Quinn's familial defenses went up.

"Before you finish that sentence, you should know some things," Quinn growled. "Dahteste is a princess of the Jicarilla Apaches, her father is Norroso Taklishin; he is the chief of his nation. My sons are princes of the Jicarilla Apache nation. They are heirs to a two hundred thousand acre cattle and horse ranch. They have never had to apologize to anyone, for anything for being who they are, and they never will. I already killed one Duncan for trying to hurt my family. Don't think I won't do that again."

Thank God for Molly's familial peacekeeping skills, otherwise she might have become a widow, right on the spot.

"Colin," Molly chastised. "You should be ashamed of yourself. Your son, to whom you taught the concept that no one was any better or worse than anyone else. You should get down on your knees to ask Dahteste and her children for forgiveness. I never thought I would say this, but I am sorry I am the wife of such a hateful, cold hearted man."

Dahteste had always assumed Quinn got his toughness from his father; obviously she was mistaken.

"Ma . . ."

"Hush, boy. I'm waiting for your father to say something . . . and it had better be the right something otherwise I will bury my son and leave here with you immediately. I can no longer live with a man who is so filled with hate and vengeance that he would turn his back on his own son."

"I no longer have a son," Colin spat. "No son of mine would kill his brother to protect an Indian squaw and her half-breed brats."

Quinn had drawn his Bowie knife and was ready to skin this father alive. Only the quick intervention of Frank and Big John holding him back, prevented the slow painful death of the elder Duncan. Through Quinn's heated blood, he could hear Dahteste's strong voice telling him to stop.

"My husband, no; there has been enough bloodshed in the Duncan family. There will be no more!"

"Alright, alright; let me go," Quinn demanded. "You will have no idea how close you came to dying today, old man. This squaw you hate so much just saved your life. Ma, we'll bury Ragan and you gather your belongings and you will come to New Mexico with us . . . we'll be your family. As for you, old man, you can stay here and rot for all I care. Frank, you and Big John are welcome to come with us."

The three men laid Ragan to rest next to his brother.

"Find peace, my brother." Quinn turned and slowly walked away.

THE TRIP WAS tiring for Molly, but exhilarating also. She had never been further than fifty miles from the farm since she had married Colin. For the first time in her life she felt free, truly alive. Her grandsons regaled their grandmother with countless stories of their father's derring-do. They pointed out all the animals they encountered and their Apache names. The boys, especially Colin, impressed Molly with the many languages they spoke. And impressed she was, if not a little trepidatious at the prospect of meeting their Jicarilla family.

"Dahteste, Quinn, thank you for giving me the chance to get to know my grandsons. You have done such a wonderful job raising your boys," Molly said. "But I am a little nervous at meeting your family, Dahteste. What must I know as not to offend you and your tradition."

"Ah, ma, don't . . ."

Dahteste intervened, yet again. "Molly, just remember you are the mother of Vo 'kohe-Nan 'kohe, White Bear; the Jicarilla respect Quinn; he is family. They will honor White Bear's mother."

"See ma, nothin' to worry about."

Both women shook their heads.

"What?"

The stagecoach rattled into La Cueva and lurched to a stop in front of the Wells Fargo office.

"Hold up there Jimmie, Jake," the driver shouted.

Smokey Randle had been driving the stage for Wells Fargo as long as there had been a stage running through La Cueva. As far as a teamster was concerned, there wasn't anyone around who could handle a six-up like Smokey. At one time, he was a darn good buckaroo, but a runaway stampede damn near killed him and ended his days as a puncher. Quinn jumped down from the driver seat, where he had been riding and helped the ladies down from the coach. At the train station in Santa Fe, Quinn had been drafted for the job of shotgun rider. Smokey's regular partner had a severe case of the brown bottle flu and was in no shape to ride shotgun. Quinn looked up at Smokey and shook his head.

"Old timer, when are you going to learn to handle a team?" Quinn joked. "I swear you hit every bump and rut between here and Santa Fe."

"Oh hell, Quinn." Smokey laughed. "I just want to give them easterners the real flavor of travelin' out here in the West."

"Well we ain't no easterners and we know you hit them damn bumps on purpose . . . ya old goat," Quinn replied.

Quinn once again turned his attention to his family. Obviously, his mother was exhausted; he half contemplated on getting a room at the hotel, then going to the ranch in the morning. But before he could move toward the rooming establishment, Flynn and Gwenny came roaring into town. They brought the entire family along to meet the elder Mrs. Duncan. Thankfully, Flynn and Hank brought horses so he and the boys could ride. Quinn had all the wagon rides he wanted; in his estimation horses were far more comfortable. For their part, the boys were ecstatic to be home.

"Papa!" the boys shouted. "There is Uncle Flynn and he brought Gus, Danny, Cochise, Benny, Beau, and Dandy. We don't have to ride in the wagon anymore!"

Along with the horses, the family consisted of Katie and Matt, Hank and Betty, and Norroso Taklishim, Itz-Chu, and Jlin Litzoque. Quinn was somewhat surprised, but happy and honored that his Apache family made the effort to come to town to meet his mother. The Apache warriors was one thing, but for the old chief to make this journey was especially gratifying. The mini family reunion was boisterous to say the least. Everyone hugged, shook hands, and clapped backs. The old chief was much more reserved and dignified. He simply raised his hand and the riotous welcome home stopped. Norroso Taklishim approached Quinn, stretching out his hands in welcome.

"Vo`kohe Nan`kohe, my son has been away long time," the chief began. "You brought my daughter and grandsons home safe. The battle Wicaso Sani sent you to do is finished. You walked path of true warrior. Now time to live in peace."

"That is my sincere wish, my father," Quinn said. "I would like you to meet my mother, Molly Duncan."

Quinn took his mother's hand and walked with her to where Norroso Taklishim stood. Quinn motioned for her to step forward and greet the old chief. Self assuredly Molly walked forward and presented herself to the Apache leader.

"Chief Norroso Taklishim, I am White Bear's mother in whom I am most proud. He has always been a good son, father, and husband . . . he will continue to do so," Molly remarked. "He has brought me here to live with him and his family. I hope to be welcome in your home as well."

Damn, Quinn thought, she is really something. The old chief was equally impressed.

"White Bear's mother will always be welcome on Apache land. You are part of Apache family. We look to future of peace and plenty. We thank White Bear for keeping Apache land safe. Now we go home; we celebrate you here."

And celebrate they did. Upon arrival at the ranch, as tired as everyone was, the family celebrated with a huge feast, singing, and dancing. Apache and white joined together in love and friendship to celebrate the return of Quinn and his family. The addition of Molly to the mixed family was certainly a bonus . . . a wonderful happenstance indeed. After two days of revelry, everyone collapsed in an exhausted heap.

Molly was given her choice of living in the house with Quinn and his family or the old homestead, which was in need of a good cleaning and airing out, but otherwise quite livable. She chose the old homestead . . . she didn't want to be underfoot. If truth be told, she would like to have a little quiet privacy; she wasn't sure she was up to living with four rambunctious boys day in day out.

The days turned into weeks and months, then years. Life on the Double D returned to normal . . . cattle and horses were born, raised, and sold. The land was revered by the family and protected from development. The town grew, then shrunk, then grew until about 1500 citizens lived within the borders of La Cueva. Molly lived with the family from her arrival in 1886 until her death ten years later on March 15, 1896. Colin Duncan had hung himself two years after Molly left him. According to Big John, hate could only sustain the old man for so long. One night, in a drunken fit, he went to the barn and tied a rope to a rafter, put the loop around his neck, then jumped from the hayloft. Quinn never told his mother the details of her husband's death, all she need know was he died. Deep down, Quinn suspected she knew he hadn't told her the whole truth, but she never said.

At fifty-eight years of age, Quinn wasn't ready to retire by any means, but the boys needed to learn to take on some of the responsibilities of running the various ranching and mining operations that made up the Duncan family business interests. Colin was going to go back East to school. He expressed an interest in becoming a doctor so he could help his people.

Quinn was sitting under the parlay tree with Flynn discussing the cattle shipment they were about to make when Colin approached the pair.

"Papa," Colin said, "I hate to interrupt, but I'd like to talk with you about school, if you have a minute."

"I always have time for you, son. Let's go for a ride so we won't be bothered," Quinn replied.

"Well, I guess I ain't invited, so I'll get back to work," Flynn huffed.

"No, you ain't invited and I wish you would get back to work," Quinn retorted.

Father and son saddled up, mounted, and galloped out if the yard.

"Papa, why do you aggravate Uncle Flynn so much?" Colin asked.

"Because there are few things I enjoy more than needling my little brother." Quinn laughed. "Of course, if he ever found out the whole point is to get a rise out of him, if I didn't, I'd probably quit. Would take all the fun out of the affair."

Colin shook his head.

"You know, mother is right. You two are like a couple of kids."

"Humph, your mother is right about a good many things." Quinn smiled. "Particularly where your uncle and I are concerned . . . now don't you go tellin' her I said this. I might lose faith in your ability to keep a confidence."

"She won't hear that from me," Colin promised.

"Now I know we aren't taking this ride for our health nor to exercise these horses," Quinn surmised. "What's on your mind?"

"Papa, I was just thinking about going back east to medical school. I want to be able to help my people; I think that is the best way," Colin said. "What do you think?"

"I might not be the best one to advise you son," Quinn whispered.

Colin looked a little confused. "Papa, you always have guided me in the right direction, all my life. Why would this be different?"

"Because, son," Quinn explained. "I was a doctor once; I vowed to do no harm . . . part of the doctor's oath. I betrayed that oath when I went to war. I could have stayed in the military hospital, but I didn't; I ran away because medicine in wartime didn't match up with my view of medicine. I couldn't cut off limbs to save a life . . . I was a butcher in a meat market, not a surgeon. I joined a calvary unit and instead of saving lives, I took lives. A little hypocritical don't you think?"

"Papa, I think you are too hard on yourself . . ."

"You been talking to your mother again?"

"No, papa, just my own observation. I will go to school; I want to be a doctor; I can help my people the most that way."

Quinn was near to bursting with pride in his son.

"I'm glad you made this decision. But you must understand that you have chosen a difficult path. For you, living in the east will be like living in a foreign country. The customs, traditions, and beliefs are strictly European in origin. To the easterners, you will be a savage; they will belittle and disrespect you and your beliefs and customs. Some may even spit on you; tell you that you don't belong in polite, civilized society. You will have to stand strong and hold onto who you are; believe in what you have been taught. But most importantly, remember you are not alone . . . your mother and I are inside you just as you are inside us."

Quinn took a bear tooth and eagle talon pendant from around his neck and placed the keepsake around his son's neck. "This has brought me good luck and kept me safe for all these years. I expect this necklace will do the same for you."

Quinn had earned these symbols of strength and bravery from a Cheyenne chief. His name was Mo'ehno'haOhvovo'haextse. Spotted Horse in English. This is when he was given his Cheyenne name . . . Vo`kohe Nan`kohe . . . White Bear.

"Thank you, papa," Colin said. "I will treasure this always. Now I must prepare for my journey. I will go say farewell to my grandfather, then I will take a ritual sweat. The train in Santa Fe going east will leave in three days. Will you, mother, and my brothers ride with me?"

"Of course," Quinn replied. "Your leaving will be hardest on your mother; she will miss you terribly."

The younger Duncan embraced his father; both men stayed in the embrace for several seconds.

"I must go and prepare for my journey," Colin said.

Then he returned to his horse and rode in the direction of the Jicarilla homeland. Flynn had walked some distance from the parlay tree, but not so far that he couldn't hear the conversation between father and son.

"This is going to be a tough row to hoe for that young man," Flynn surmised. "But if anyone can do what he has in mind, Colin can. He has yours and Dahteste's blood running in his veins; he also has your single minded toughness. He'll be alright."

"I don't doubt his abilities and toughness," Quinn replied, "I worry about the reception he's going to get . . . and four years is a long time to be away from home."

"I know if I tell you not to worry, you will anyway," Flynn remarked, "but you'll see, things will be okay."

"My head says you're right," Quinn allowed, "but my heart isn't as sure, brother. Let's have some Scotch whiskey; maybe I can forget my son is leaving in three days."

"Sounds like a good idea to me," Flynn agreed.

Gwenny and Dahteste were sitting on the porch snapping string beans during the conversation between the three men. Dahteste watched as Quinn disappeared into the house to retrieve his favorite drink. She watched while he walked back to the parlay tree where his brother waited patiently.

"I wish I knew what that whole thing was about," Gwenny noted. "Don't you?"

Dahteste thought a moment, then replied, "I know already. My son will be leaving on a long journey very soon and will not return for many years."

Gwenny was shocked at the news. "How do you know that, for sure. We couldn't hear them from here."

"Did you see my husband give Colin his pendant?" Dahteste asked.

"Yes," Gwenny whispered.

"That pendant means more to Quinn than any possession he has. He would not give the bear claw and eagle talon to anyone, except his first born son. The talisman has great power to protect Colin on this perilous journey. And now my husband will drink the Scotch whiskey to try to dull the pain of loss. When he finds the drink that robs the senses does him no good, he will come to me."

"Men," Gwenny observed. "When will they ever understand that their wives are better prepared to help them over rough spots in life than liquor."

Both women laughed.

"Men hard-headed and stubborn. Too proud to ask woman for help," Dahteste allowed.

A thought occurred to Gwenny at that moment.

"Dahteste," Gwenny declared, "Quinn has an excuse; Flynn doesn't."

"I found, living with Quinn, white men don't need excuse to drink." Dahteste laughed.

"Very true," Gwenny agreed, "so I guess we have the chore of making sure they don't hurt themselves in the end."

Three days seemed to race by. Colin prepared himself all he could for the impending journey. He had said his farewells to his Apache family, his uncle, and his cousins. Now the time had come for the last horseback ride he would take in his New Mexico homeland for at least four years. He specifically asked that only his parents and brothers ride with him to Santa Fe. The farewell he would make at the train station was a private affair, even sacred.

Riding the Appaloosa he and his family raised they could easily traverse the twenty some odd miles in a few hours, but Colin wanted to stretch out the time, so he set a slow, easy pace. His brothers, on the other hand, wanted to race a ways. Always a competitive bunch, Colin acquiesced and joined his three brothers in what would very likely be their last race for some time. The boys' parents, not to be left out, joined in the contest.

"Just how many miles will this race be and what will be the finish line?" Quinn asked.

"How 'bout down to Hay's Creek? That's roughly three miles," Conner said.

"Alright," Quinn shouted, "I'll see you boys when you get there . . . you too, woman."

And with that, Quinn spurred up his Appy stud and left his family in the dust. Dahteste rode close behind him.

"Damn them," young Flynn grossed. "When will we learn?"

The four boys started their horses in a flurry of dust and shouting and hurried after their parents. By the time the boys caught up Quinn was barreling down the trail within sight of the creek. Dahteste had vanished . . . she was nowhere in sight.

"Look out, papa," Ragan shouted, "I'm coming up behind you."

"Like hell you are," Connor yelled. "I will get to the creek before both of you!"

"Don't be so sure," Colin called out, "I'll be the winner today!"

The men had forgotten about Dahteste and when the five of them thundered to the creek's edge, there was Dahteste casually leaning against a tree while her horse took a well-deserved drink from the cold creek water.

"Boys," Quinn sighed, "we have been bested by the better rider on this day."

"Or any other day as well, husband." Dahteste grinned.

As for the boys, they hung their heads in defeat and went about taking care of the horses. Quinn noticed the boys' body language and took them to task.

"No sons of mine will drop their heads and slink around like lizards," Quinn rebuked. "You lost a race to a better and worthy opponent. You will honor her in her victory and not feel sorry for yourselves."

"You are right, papa," Colin said. "We are sorry mother that we dishonored you. Evidently we are not grown men yet."

"My sons, you are closer to manhood than you think," Dahteste said quietly. "You must be reminded at times to do the right thing. We all need to be reminded sometimes," she continued looking straight at Quinn.

Quinn cleared his throat audibly.

"Yes, well that was a good race anyway."

As much as Colin wanted to prolonged the inevitable, before sundown the family reached the outskirts of Santa Fe. The train's departure was set for seven in the evening, so the family would have time for a good meal and Colin could change into his new suit for the train ride. While the rest of the family ordered dinner, Colin went to the washroom to change. And change he did. When he emerged, the Colin the family knew had totally vanished and in place of a strong Apache, an easterner remained. He had cut his long hair and with the new suit, Colin looked like a different person altogether. Ragan snickered once, but a stern stare from his father put an end to any nonsense.

"Son, you look like a proper gentleman," Quinn said. "You will fit in back east with the other incoming students."

"Papa," Colin groaned, "I feel silly dressed like this and with short hair."

"My son," Dahteste said softly, "outward appearance does not change who you are here." She placed her hand on his heart. "Remember always who you are inside."

"I will mother," Colin replied.

Colin's brothers shook his hand and wished him luck.

"Try to stay out of trouble, brother. But if you can't avoid a fight remember you represent this family, so make sure you win," Conner declared.

The other brothers chimed in their agreement.

"Yeah," Flynn added. "Don't let the other guy get in the first punch."

Quinn decided he'd better regain parental control.

"Boys, Colin's priority is to get through medical school; to become a doctor, not get into fights," Quinn remarked. "Make sure you remember that, son . . . but don't let anyone get away with disrespecting you either."

"I'll remember, papa."

The train lumbered and chugged into the station. All the preparations Colin had made must now serve him well all during the quest he was about to undertake. Now was not the time to second guess his decision; there was no turning back. No matter how difficult, no matter the struggle, he must break through every obstacle in order to help his people. He embraced his mother and father and shook hands with his brothers one last time, then he boarded the train and disappeared from view. Dahteste could hold back her tears no longer; her body heaved from the heavy sobs. Quinn wrapped his strong arms around his wife in order to comfort her.

"Woman," Quinn whispered, "our son is a strong man and must walk his path alone and will be even stronger."

Strong indeed; Colin had no idea just how strong he was and the four years he was to be gone would pass by quickly. His quest would be successful and he would return home a doctor. Medical school was not without hardship. But he dealt with each difficulty with strength and dignity. Never once did he lose the respect of his peers or teachers. He learned everything he needed to know and perhaps more importantly, he taught others about Apache culture, spiritualism, and the healing properties of various plants and herbs. Folks were impressed, that's for dang sure.

Unfortunately, for Colin's family in New Mexico, the four years seemed to drag by. They felt as though time stopped . . . the world stopped turning. Had not the seasons continue to change one would think time, indeed, had stopped. However, the family was nothing if not resilient . . . they bucked up and went on with their lives. After all, the horses and cattle wouldn't take care of themselves. And, in addition, Quinn had a new headache to worry about after Ragan found gold in Hay's Creek. The young man had been moving some cattle from one pasture to another and stopped to water himself and his horse. While he was lying flat on the ground with his head in the water, he noticed something shiny in the creek bed. Sure enough he found gold; quite a bit, as a matter of fact . . . two handfuls of good sized gold nuggets.

"Well I'll be damned, Apache," Ragan declared. "Lookie what I got here; this here is gold. I don't know if I should be glad or not. Papa will not be happy if word of this gets out. We better go tell him before some fool stumbles onto our land and finds this. C'mon, boy, let's go."

Ragan leapt into the saddle and encouraged Apache to run as fast as he could. Quinn hated to see the boys run their horses and there was always hell to pay if they did. But under the circumstances, Ragan figured his father would make allowances. Ragan rode Apache into the yard at the same time hollering at the top of his lungs. "Papa, mother, come quick!"

Quinn came crashing out of the barn while Dahteste ran from the house.

"Boy, you better have a good reason for runnin' that horse that way," Quinn scolded.

"Look, papa! Look what I found in Hay's Creek," the boy cried breathlessly.

Ragan pulled his fancy rag out of this saddlebag and unwrapped the golden treasure, or curse depending on your point of view.

"Damn," Quinn breathed. "Does anyone else know about this? You didn't say anything to anyone did you?"

"No, sir. There weren't nobody else around and I came straight here," Ragan pledged.

"That's good," Quinn acknowledged.

Dahteste knew from experience what gold fever meant. She saw Native lands overrun, then stolen by crazed prospectors.

"What will be do, husband?" Dahteste asked.

"Nothin'," Quinn announced. "We'll have a family meeting. We sure as hell don't need any more money, and we sure as hell don't want people stompin' around on our range lookin' for gold. This will be our secret. You did the right thing, son. Now go cool out that horse."

That evening, the entire family gathered in Quinn and Dahteste's living room to discuss Ragan's discovery. Quinn sent Ragan over to get Matt and Katie and Hank and Betty. They needed to be apprised of the situation; especially Hank and Betty since their ranch sat on the other end of Hay's Creek. For all they knew, the whole damn creek could be full of that damn stuff.

"Alright, big brother. What's so damned important that required a big ol' family meetin'," Flynn grumbled.

Quinn dropped the rag containing the gold in Flynn's lap.

"Lord a'mighty," Flynn whistled, "where in the hell did you find these?"

"I didn't, Ragan did . . . in Hay's Creek," Quinn said.

"Where abouts, boy?" Flynn demanded.

"Don't matter where," Quinn interrupted. "The fewer people know, the better."

"You mean to tell me you ain't even gonna tell your own brother?" Flynn was insulted.

"I wouldn't even tell my own mother, God rest her," Quinn affirmed. "'Sides, I don't know; Ragan never said exactly where. Anyway, that's beside the point. The most important thing is that no one else learns about this, otherwise we'll play hell tryin' to keep every gold huntin' fool off our property."

"Papa," Conner questioned, "if Ragan is the only one who knows, why do we have to do anything? We don't let people on our property anyway. How would anybody else find out?"

"Just the way Ragan did, son," Quinn pointed out. "Simply by accident. If one of the hands stops to get a drink or water his horse, and finds more gold, what's to keep him from tellin' everybody in town when he goes to the saloon on Saturday night."

"Greed," Katie said. "Why would he tell anyone else? Wouldn't he want to keep all the gold for himself?"

"If he got drunk enough, and he wanted to impress a saloon girl, he'd be apt to say most anything," Quinn explained.

"Well, then, what will we do, papa?" Lil Flynn asked.

"Tomorrow, Ragan and I are gonna take a ride along Hays's Creek to see just exactly where and how much gold is there," Quinn said.

"Hank, I want you to scour your end of Hay's Creek. Who knows, the whole damn creek might be full of this stuff. If that's the case, I don't know what the hell we'll do," Quinn admitted.

Every member of the family spent all their spare time and the better part of a month scouring the waters of Hay's Creek looking for, and hoping not to find, gold. The younger Flynn found the honey hole. Much to Quinn's chagrin, there was a large deposit of gold about mile upstream from where Ragan found the original nuggets. Quinn figured they washed downstream during high water. A plan was set in place to hide the large deposit. Quinn decided to cover the creek with fallen trees. They would be arranged in such a way as to look like they fell over the creek without damming the creek. The elder Flynn was a little dubious Quinn's plan would work.

"That is the most ridiculous thing I ever heard tell of. How you gonna make trees fall over the creek so's they look natural?"

"Well, I'll tell you, little brother," Quinn explained, "we're gonna set charges small enough to bring down the trees, but not so large as to blow the trees all to hell."

"And you think that will work, papa?" Ragan asked.

"Yep," Quinn said. "We did something similar during the war to block trails to make life hell for Confederate troops trying to get from one place to another. If we're lucky, the trees will hide the gold cash, or at the very least make prospecting for the damn stuff too hard to bother with."

"Okay, big brother. You're the boss; let's get to work."

"The sooner the better, Flynn. Oh, by the way," Quinn added, "let me have those nuggets Ragan found."

"How come?" Flynn asked innocently. "What's a handful of nuggets in this overall scheme of yours?"

"Think about what gold causes. All people would need to crawl all over our ranchland are a few gold nuggets. They'd figure where there's some, there's bound to be more. Besides, what's a man as rich as you are need with a couple hundred dollars worth of gold?" Quinn said.

Flynn looked like he was being robbed of his last dime.

"You have to admit, Uncle Flynn, papa's got a point," Conner agreed.

Gwenny's well placed elbow in Flynn's ribs forced him to give up the goods.

"I guess you all are right. But this still doesn't make me feel any better," Flynn complained.

The next day Quinn, Hank, Conner, and Ragan went down to the creek to set the charges. Once all the explosives were placed correctly, Quinn set off the dynamite. The trees fell in a random fashion across the creek just as Quinn had predicted. Not only that, the water flow wasn't slowed appreciably.

"There ya are, boys, job done," Quinn boasted, "and nothin's the worse for wear."

"Well I'll be damned, Uncle Quinn," Hank observed. "In the beginnin', I wasn't convinced your plan would work, but you sure proved me wrong."

The Duncan brothers all grinned.

"You been hangin' around your pa too much, Hank." Conner chuckled.

A quizzical look appeared on Hank's race.

"Well, who else am I supposed to hang around with if not pa?" Hank asked.

"Your ma," Ragan suggested. "She has more common sense."

"She married pa, didn't she? That shows she musta thought he was worthwhile," Hank countered.

"Yeah, he's . . ."

Quinn cut Lil Flynn off in mid-sentence. "That's enough pickin' on Flynn. He's family. We don't make fun of family and he's my little brother. I'll take on anyone . . . anyone . . . who defames my brother. Besides, he's a good, brave man who would give his life for each and every one of you, don't ever forget that."

"We know, papa. We were just having a little fun," Ragan said. "I apologize, Hank, to you and your pa."

"Yeah," the brothers said.

"We didn't mean no harm," Conner added. "Papa's right; ya don't make fun of family."

WITH THE POTENTIAL gold crisis averted, the Duncan clan settled back into their daily routine. Three months had passed since Colin's departure to the east. Thanksgiving was on the horizon as well as another New Mexico winter. The wedding anniversaries for Katie and Hank would be celebrated on Thanksgiving as well as celebrating another successful fall cattle auction. The younger Duncans each had growing families . . . their children were all school age. Still there was a kind of hole in the middle of the celebration preparations . . . the eldest Duncan son . . . Colin . . . was missing. No matter how hard she tried, Dahteste couldn't throw herself into the joy of the season. Quinn tried to cheer up his wife as best he could.

"Wife, I haven't seen you truly happy for months," Quinn observed. "Not even when little Carrie's goat butted Flynn so hard he landed in the water trough."

Dahteste allowed herself a slight smile at the memory.

"Yes, Katie's daughter has her mother's ability to make mischief."

Carrie was supposed to keep the goat penned up, but she let him out just as Flynn was bending over to pick up a nail. The goat did what goats do naturally and sent Flynn flying into the water trough. The smile, however, was fleeting.

"Aahh, Dahteste," Quinn whispered, "I wish you would snap out of this. I never thought you would be so mournful when Colin went back east."

"Husband,"Dahteste cried, "he is my first born. The bond is strongest with the first."

"I know," Quinn sighed, "I miss him too, but he wouldn't want us to be so sad. Please, for our son's sake, will you try to cheer up . . . and for me also?"

Dahteste turned to face her husband. "I will try. A ritual sweat will take the impurities from my body. Prayers to the Creator will heal my spirit."

Quinn kissed his wife tenderly, then she walked to the sweat lodge to begin her ritual. She would sweat, fast, and pray for three days. Then only time would tell if Dahteste would be well. Quinn wasn't the best at figuring out women's problems, so he went to see Gwenny. He found her working in her flower bed.

"Gwenny, I swear between you and Dahteste, I don't know who grows the prettiest flowers," Quinn gushed. "Everyone in the county just goes on and on about your garden."

Gwenny was really good at cutting through false praise the Duncan boys were famous for.

"Quinn Duncan." Gwenny laughed. "I wish you'd remember I'm married to a Duncan. I know what blarney is and when all this praise is heaped on me, I get suspicious. What did you do now that you shouldn't have?"

Quinn blushed, looked down at this boots, and shuffled his feet like a six year old who got caught with his hand in the cookie jar.

"Gwenny," Quinn admitted, "I don't know why I try. But I didn't do anything, for a change. I'm worried about Dahteste; she misses Colin something awful. I don't know what to do; she's performing a ritual sweat now. I hope this helps, but if she keeps on like this, her grief will kill her before Colin gets home."

Gwenny nodded in agreement. "I know, Quinn. I've noticed her grieving too. I'll be glad to talk to her when she finishes her ritual. We'll be working on the quilt for the Thanksgiving raffle. That will be a good time to talk."

Quinn gave Gwenny a hug.

"Thank you, Gwenny, I'm beholdin' to you."

"Nonsense, Quinn. That's what families are for . . . to help each other out when needed."

"Well thanks just the same," Quinn said. And as he turned to go, added, "Brrr, turnin' cold. We'll have our first snow 'fore long."

"I think you're right," Gwenny agreed. "Our old aching bones are telling us bad weather is on the horizon."

Quinn felt a might bit relieved knowing Gwenny would have a talk with Dahteste. He just hoped his wife's stoic Apache character didn't stop her from opening up to her best friend. There was still enough work to be done getting the livestock ready for the coming winter months to take his mind off Dahteste's troubles for a bit. The hay barns were filled, but the hay needed to be delivered to the cattle and horses out in the pastures. Although the ranch was located lower down in the foothills of the Sangre de Cristo Mountains, the annual snowfall could reach four or five feet. As far as he was concerned, Quinn figured that was more than enough snow. To borrow a nautical phrase . . . "all hands on deck" would be needed to get the work done. Quinn walked down to the bunk house to meet Flynn and Hank to divvy up the workload.

Quinn wasn't the only one beefing about the cold weather.

"Dang, brother," Flynn remarked, "I don't think I remember the temperature falling this fast this early in the season before, do you?"

"I think you're right," Quinn agreed, "this winter could be downright dangerous if we aren't careful. I've decided to move the cattle and horses into Red Rock Canyon. There is good forage there and there'll be a better windbreak than being out on pasture. And Red Rock is closer to the main headquarters . . . that means a shorter distance to haul hay. What do you two think?"

"I think that's a good idea," Hank replied, "but we better get them moved before the snow hits."

"Yeah," Flynn concurred, "and we could get snow anytime now."

"Good," Quinn said. "Since we're all agreed, let's get started today."

"You bet," Flynn said, "the sooner the better."

The buckaroos were all gathered around the stove, but they heard most of the conversation between the Duncans. One by one, they got up, put their coffee cups down, and turned their attention to the head Duncan.

"Fellas," Quinn began, "I'm sure you heard all or most of our conversation. We've got a whole helluva lot of work to do and we have to get started today . . . before the weather turns bad. One thing though: I want you all to understand that a steer or horse's life isn't more important than any one of you. Work carefully out there and don't let yourself get in a bad spot that might cause a wreck. You all know your jobs, so I don't have to tell what to do. We'll start east on Hank's place and move everything west to Red Rock. The Jicarilla and I will handle rounding up the horses; Flynn and Hank will take you boys and get the cattle moving. Take all the time you need, but be efficient. We want to make sure we get all the cattle moved."

Quinn paused for a minute, then continued. "Ben, I want you and Joey to pick up the salt and move all you can to the canyon," he ordered. "That way, the cattle will move to the salt blocks. If you need more, there is plenty in the store room. All right. Are there any questions?"

No one said a word.

"Good, let's get moving," Quinn commanded.

The Double D holdings took in nearly half a million acres. Of course, not all of that acreage was pasture for livestock. Nonetheless, the hands needed to cover an incredibly huge area to get all the cattle found and rounded up before the snows came. Quinn's passion was raising fine working stock horses, preferably Appaloosas, so he would lead the Jicarilla vaqueros in gathering and bringing in all the ranch horses. The entire operation was going to take the better part of a month, by the time the herds were rounded up, doctored, and branding any animal that was missed in the spring branding. There would be no kidding anyone involved; a great deal of hard work would be required to get the job done. There was going to be one very important person joining the roundup—Dahteste. Quinn was hoping the hard work would take her mind off her absentee son; at least for a while. His wife would join him and the other vaqueros after she finished her rituals. And not long after the work began, Quinn spied Dahteste loping her stallion through the grassy meadow.

"Good morning, wife." Quinn smiled. "How are you feeling this fine autumn morning?"

"I am well, husband," she replied. "For the first time in a long while. My spirit is whole and at peace."

"You have no idea how happy I am to hear that." Quinn sighed. "I was worried, but I knew you had to find your way back to us on your own. I felt helpless," he admitted.

"I am sorry I caused your heavy heart, husband. I miss my first born. I felt my heart ripped from my body. But I have healed my body and soul. I know I will see my son again and until then, life must go on," Dahteste deduced.

"You are wise and strong, wife," Quinn said. "I love you and I am proud you are my wife."

"I am glad you are my husband. Now we must work."

Dahteste galloped off to cut off a few strays and drive them back to the herd. Quinn moved up to his position on the left side of the herd, smiling all the while. Conner and Ragan were happy to have their mother back where she belonged as well. The young men rode over to greet her.

"Mother," they said, "we're glad to see you out of the house." Dahteste smiled.

"We were scared you would be sick," Ragan said.

"Truly, mother," Conner added, "we didn't know how to help you so we prayed and offered gifts to the Creator to make you spirit whole again."

"Thank you, my sons," Dahteste replied. "I felt your power during my sweat. That knowledge helped to bring me back from the realm of the dead. I will not go there again."

With two weeks of hard work from before sunup until after sundown, the Duncan roundup ended, successfully. Now everyone could slow down and relax for a bit. Thanksgiving was approaching as well as celebrating two wedding anniversaries; there was lots to do and everyone pitched in to get the food and the setting just right. Both couples decided to renew their vows at the spring where they were married. All parties involved were hoping for snow to make the renewal as close as possible to the original ceremony. No one was disappointed . . . the night before the ceremony, a heavy snow fell all night long.

The only variation on the theme this time round was instead of a preacher, Norroso Taklishim would officiate the renewal. This would probably be the last time the old chief would take part in any official ceremony. He was nearing his ninety-sixth year and was becoming more and more feeble. Still his mind was sharp and his keen eyes saw things most of the young ones couldn't. However, the day-to-day running of tribal duties had been turned over to his eldest son Itz-Chu. His youngest son, Jlin-Litzque was made sub-chief . . . he was in charge of the herds of cattle and horses belonging to the Jicarilla. He also oversaw the men who cared for the herds. He worked closely with the Duncan brothers to make sure the herds were viable and healthy.

Anyway, the renewal ceremony and the Thanksgiving celebration went off without a hitch. Flynn's best friend was his bottle of twenty-year-old scotch whiskey which he imported, several cases at a time . . . at considerable cost, from Edinburgh, Scotland. Still Flynn, for the most part, was an amiable character and shared his valuable commodity with family and friends. Gwenny kept a close watch over her imbibing husband in case he got too carried away. He'd been known to make rather dangerous challenges when he was under the influence. No one wanted anyone injured by foolish shenanigans.

"I swear," Gwenny lamented, "that man would drink the Pecos River dry if it were filled with scotch."

Quinn nodded. "Yeah, that's the curse of the folks from the Highlands. They all love their whiskey. Thankfully, Flynn doesn't do this too often. He always swears, after enduring a fierce hangover, he'll never get drunk again. I wish I had a nickel for every time he swears off the liquor."

Both got a chuckle from that pronouncement. Quinn bid his sister-in-law goodbye and went off to mingle with the other guests. He especially wanted to wish Katie and Matt all the best for Katie was the first of Gwenny's children to welcome him into the family and from that time on, they shared a special relationship. Quinn encouraged Katie to take on jobs that were traditionally held by men. He taught her to train horses, handle both a Colt 45 and a Winchester rifle, and skin out deer and antelope. He taught her and Colin the practice of medicine, both white and Native practices. He knew she had a head for figures, so he and Flynn decided she should keep the Duncan holdings accounts. But most of all he loved her like the daughter he and Dahteste never had.

"Hey there, young lady," Quinn called. "Congratulations to both of you . . . how long have you two been married . . . ten years, right?"

"That's right, Mr. Duncan," Matt replied politely.

Quinn shook his head.

"Katie, what's the matter with that husband of yours? After this long, you'd think he'd quit callin' me mister . . . makes me feel old. Quinn would do just fine."

"Uncle Quinn." Katie laughed. "I've been trying to get him to stop, but he seems to be intimidated by you."

"Well now that's just plain silly." Quinn chuckled. "However did you come to be intimidated by me, boy?"

"Sir, I mean Quinn," Matt stammered. "I guess I can't get over seeing you take on those five rustlers, single-handedly, some years back. That made quite an impression on me; I decided I'd better stay on your good side . . . especially since I was going to marry Katie. I know how much you care about her welfare."

"Why, son, that was eleven years ago!" Quinn roared. "You mean to tell me you been scared of me that long?"

"Yes, Uncle Quinn," Katie said. "You certainly made an impression on my husband; you still do . . . both of us, I might add."

"Is that how you come to name your first born after me?" Quinn asked.

"That was one reason. The other is we want our son, well, all our children for that matter, to know you and be proud to be a member of the Duncan clan. Blood kin or not, you will always be part of our family, just as we are a part of yours."

Quinn was really touched. So much so, he had to turn away to wipe a tear from the corner of his eye.

"Thank you Katie." Quinn smiled. "You have always been nothing but a source of pride to me . . . both of you . . . and I'm proud and happy to be your uncle."

And that is pretty much how 1896 ended . . . a huge Duncan family get together. Christmas and the New Year celebrations were rather anticlimactic. The winter was pretty fierce and long, but that past too and spring of 1897 brought a fresh new start for another year.

"C'MON, WOMAN," QUINN growled, "that dang train will be rollin' in pretty soon. Ain't you about ready yet?"

"Husband," Dahteste smiled, "I want to look my best for my son's homecoming. When will you ever learn patience?"

Quinn couldn't help but smile. Dahteste turned sixty this year, but you'd never know her age just by looking. The only concession to age was a streak of grey in her jet black hair. She still stood straight and tall; her visage was striking to say the least. Time had been kind to Quinn as well. At sixty-two, Quinn cut quite a large figure and no one, unless they had a death wish, wanted to take him on.

"As always, wife, you are right. And don't worry about not looking your best. You are still as beautiful as the day I asked you father for your hand in marriage. Age hasn't touched you unkindly; you have a beauty that only comes with living a long life . . . and we still have many years yet to spend together."

"I know that, Quinn," Dahteste replied. "We have already lived long enough to see our grandchildren. We have had a good life."

A good life for sure. The turn of the century had brought many changes to the world in which the Duncans lived. The Wells Fargo stage line was nearly a thing of the past. The train came into La Cueva and there were even paved sidewalks and electricity in town. There were even one or two families who drove one of those new-fangled motor cars. The Duncans no longer had to drive their herds to Santa Fe and beyond to sell them; they simply brought them to town and loaded them on to stock cars to points north and east. Conner, at twenty-one, was married and had one child, a son named August (Gus). Ragan and Flynn were dating, but showed no interest in settling down and getting married.

"Marriage is for married folks," Flynn announced at dinner one evening, "and I sure ain't interested in bein' one of those yet."

Ragan seconded that pronouncement.

"That's for dang sure. I haven't even seen the world yet. No way I'm ready for marrying."

"You plan on seein' the world do ya, son?" Quinn asked.

"I dunno," Ragan replied. "I ain't never been anywhere further away than Denver when we went to the livestock show."

"What about that trip back east to Gettysburg?" Conner asked.

"We were just kids then," Ragan countered. "That don't count."

Yes, the year 1900 brought many changes, for sure, but the best change was Colin was finished with medical school and would be returning home on the evening train. Once again, Quinn asked his wife if she was ready to go.

"I am ready, my husband," Dahteste said.

"Okay, I'll have Conner bring the carriage around."

"No!" Dahteste ordered. "I will ride Pecos to meet my son."

Quinn should have known better. Dahteste was dressed in her finest riding gear: a brocade vaquero jacket, black split skirt pants, soft black leather boots, a white blouse turquoise scarf, and necklace. Her strikingly shiny, black hair was tied back in one long single braid. On her boots she wore her silver inlaid Mexican spurs. She wanted Pecos to be well dressed also. He was wearing his finest turquoise and white saddle pad under the hand-tooled Charro saddle with turquoise inlays in the horn, pommel, and cantle. She mounted with ease, belying her sixty years. Her black Appaloosa with a brilliant white blanket pranced in anticipation of the ride to town. Pecos seemed to understand the importance of this trip to town and intended to display a dazzling, eye catching presence.

While the Duncan men put on their Sunday finest, Quinn couldn't help but observe . . .

"Dang, woman, I feel slightly underdressed next to you. What do you think boys? Is not your mother the finest looking lady in all of the territory of New Mexico; heck, in the whole wide world even?"

"Yes, papa," Conner agreed, "she is indeed."

Since Dahteste was riding, the whole family was horseback. Quinn led Colin's horse Arapaho; the family would see how rusty Colin was when he got on his horse.

Conner's wife, Margarette, was mounted as well. She carried Gus in a cradle board, just as she did when working cattle. The hands would often hear the toddler squealing and laughing at the top of his lungs while Margarette galloped over the prairie chasing a maverick steer. She was from an old well-respected Spanish family. At first, she had a difficult time fitting into the boisterous, fun loving Duncan family, considering her family was much more formal and reserved. In her family, women were expected to be dutiful wives and daughters. The Duncan family was quite different in that women were on par with men. In fact, they were expected to compete and beat the men in just about every endeavor. Now after two years, she could ride and work cattle with the best of the men.

The sun was dipping below the horizon by the time the family arrived at the train stop. As usual, the presence of the Duncan family in town was cause for quite a stir. People on the streets stopped what they were doing just to look. People could be seen staring out of windows. On this occasion, the gossip mongers had Colin coming home today.

The anticipation and excitement of the train's impending arrival was almost palatable. What seemed like forever, the sound of the train's engine could be heard in the distance. Then the smoke from the stack could be seen above the trees and lastly the train came into view, chugging laboriously up the final incline into town. Quinn and Dahteste had dismounted and waited on the platform for Colin to disembark from the first passenger car. The young boy who got onto the train four long years ago was no more. Instead a tall, strong young man emerged to greet his parents and brothers. His brothers expected to be able to razz Colin about his dude clothes, but were disappointed to see he had changed into the trappings of a rancher who had simply been away on a business trip. Dahteste was beside herself and ran to embrace her son. Tears flowed freely from mother and son; Margarette was equally touched; even his tough brothers were overcome with emotion. Only Quinn was able to hold onto his emotions, but just barely. Dahteste spoke first.

"My son, my heart is full of joy at your return," she cried. "I have missed you terribly these four long years. There was a hole in my heart and my soul was sick. Now all of me is healed."

'Mother," Colin replied, "I have missed you too. I am not ashamed to admit I cried myself to sleep for the first month." He turned to his father. "I know my father is ashamed of me for such an admission, but I couldn't help myself."

"Colin, there is nothing you could do to make me ashamed of you. And since we're being honest, I shed a tear or two myself."

Colin made the rounds to greet his brothers and meet his new young nephew.

"Conner, I see many things have changed since I've been away. Nice to meet you Margarette and your young son. I'm glad you were able to tame this wild brother of mine."

"I'm pleased to meet you as well. I've heard many stories of your many exploits," Margarette replied.

"My many exploits?" Colin laughed. "You and I must sit down and have a long talk about exploits."

Colin turned to his other two brothers and embraced them. There were a few jokes and much laughter between the brothers. Colin hadn't realized just how much he missed his family until this moment. He turned to his father and looked over Quinn's shoulder. There was Apache waiting patiently to get patted and scratched by his friend. Quinn handed the reins over to his son. The Appaloosa stallion was the herd sire for Colin's small herd. He had been working hard to build up a medium sized breeding operation to provide good stock horses for the ranch, as well as building up foundation Appaloosas to help rebuild the breed. Fortunately, Quinn was able to get some quality horses from the Nez Perce before the 1877 war. After their defeat, the Indians horses were either killed or commandeered by the US Army effectively ending the Nez Perce ability to carry on the war or escape to Canada. Apache was a full brother to Pecos and the son of Quinn's stallion Commander. Colin touched heads with his horse, his partner. He rubbed the stallion's neck and spoke a soft greeting to his friend.

"Papa, thank you for bringing him to town," Colin said. "I was so excited to see him again. The trip home in a wagon would have been almost too much."

Colin swung himself deftly into the saddle. The Apache were known for their expertise in horsemanship both in battle and on the hunt. Their horses were as strong and powerful as their riders; they were the most feared light cavalry unit in the Southwest . . . probably on the plains as well. The citizens of La Cueva were in for a rollicking exit of the Duncan clan with Colin leading the way.

"C'mon, everybody! Let's go home!" Colin shouted.

The citizens of La Cueva joined in on the shouting and yahooing emanating from the Duncan clan. Clouds of dust roiled up from the street caused by the horses' thundering hooves striking the ground. If there were any strangers in town, they would have thought La Cueva was the most uncivilized town in the west. The rowdy exhibition by the Duncan clan notwithstanding, the town's first family was responsible for all the modern development in La Cueva, decent treatment of the Apache, and peace between the Apache and whites for nearly twenty-five years. In fact, with Colin's return, the Apache and the town's citizens would have a doctor. Quinn had served as the only doctor between La Cueva and Santa Fe. In case of emergencies, Quinn was more than able to intervene whenever the occasion arose; but now, both the Jicarilla and La Cueva had a full time doctor.

After the initial stampede out of town, the family slowed down to a brisk ground covering walk. This gave Colin a chance to talk with his parents.

"Mother, papa," Colin began. "I can't tell you how much I love you both. They say you never know how much you love and need someone until they are out of reach. There were times I wanted to quit and come home."

"Why didn't you?" Quinn asked.

"I figured I would shame you and the family name," Colin said softly. "More than anything, I wanted to prove to myself I could compete with whites students. I told myself I had to be strong and see my journey through to the end."

"And you did, my son," Dahteste said. "Also you finished at the top of your class. That is remarkable, but I knew you would. I prayed and fasted until I had a vision. I saw you getting praise from your teachers. I knew then you succeeded and you would be coming home."

Quinn was a little surprised.

"Wife, you never told me that," Quinn remarked.

"Yes, husband. Just before the roundup after I fasted in the sweat hut. I had this vision," Dahteste explained.

"I'll be damned." Quinn grinned. "Once again Apache spiritualism proves to be true. I'll never doubt that again."

"You shouldn't, papa," Colin observed, "as many times you've had visions that come to fruition."

"You're right, son, absolutely right."

The rest of the ride home the family exchanged good-humored conversation. They shared memories and future plans now that Colin was home. The family was whole again; there were no worries, nothing ominous on the horizon. Dahteste, especially, was glad; still she wouldn't be totally at peace until they rode through the gate at the home place.

Once he unpacked and stowed away his belongings, handed out presents he brought his family, and finished dinner, Colin felt as though a heavy weight had been lifted from his shoulders. He stood alone on the front porch, watching the sun dip below the horizon. The western sky was a brilliant mixed palette of red, orange, black, and blue. This time of the day, Colin figured the Creator must be sitting down enjoying a nice long rest after another enormously busy day. This was a signal to all humans to stop and take stock in all the blessings they had; all the things for which they should be thankful. The sound of jingling spurs and footfalls on the wooden porch interrupted Colin's thoughts. His father arrived with a bottle of Flynn's scotch and two glasses.

"Good to have you home, boy. Here, have a drink and we can do some thinkin' drinkin'."

Quinn gestured to the parlay tree where both men could sit and converse about everything and nothing. Quinn poured out two glasses of scotch and handed one to Colin whose gaze had returned to the setting sun.

"That view never gets old, does it, son," Quinn observed.

"No, papa," Colin replied. "There were times when the only thing that kept me going was visualizing this view. I'd close my eyes and this scene appeared. I agree, papa, I'm so glad to be home."

"I don't want to rush you, but now that you are home, what are your plans?" Quinn queried.

"I need to get re-acclimated to being home; that may take a week or two. I want to oversee the building of the hospital on Jicarilla land, and setting up an office in town. While that's going on, I want to get back to working with my Appaloosas."

"That sounds reasonable, but there's one thing. The hospital is already built; at least the framework and the rooms. We didn't do much inside 'cause we figured you'd want to set things up to suit yourself. We can take a ride over there tomorrow, if you want."

"Papa, I don't know what to say!" Colin exclaimed. "This is great news."

"Good, I'm glad you're okay with us goin' ahead and buildin' your hospital, but we figured you'd want to get started as quick as you could. We just speeded up the process is all."

"Papa, I can't wait to see what you did. I feel like I did when I was a kid . . . waiting for Christmas morning to open presents," Colin proclaimed.

"I'm glad you're okay with this." Quinn sighed. "I just didn't want you think I was taking over."

"Papa, this is going to be the biggest challenge I've ever had. Believe me when I say, I'll take all the help you have to give."

And help he got . . . the entire Duncan clan pitched in whenever Colin needed help. The Jicarilla tribe knew this hospital with white medicine would help them, so they helped their adopted son. There were some that were a little skeptical about white man's medicine, especially the elders, but eventually they came around too. Colin was wise enough to understand that much of Apache healing could be added to his medical practice and benefit all his patients. Colin taught several young men who were interested in learning medical practices. In addition, he also taught both young men and women to be nurses and midwives. All the while Colin was at medical school, he never forgot who he was and where he came from. He honored his heritage in everything he did. With that in mind, he named the hospital The Wicaso Sani Jicarilla Hospital. This would be a place of healing where all people Indian, Mexican, or white could come whenever they needed help. The office in town was named La Cueva Apothecary. Folks all around could come in to see the doctor and get medicines for all kinds of illnesses. Colin's vision of helping people who needed a doctor was well on its way to becoming a reality.

WORLD WAR I, the war to end all wars ended in 1918. Eighteen years had passed since Colin came home from the east. The Duncan clan had been so prosperous and happy for over forty-five years. The Duncan holdings continued to expand to include mining and lumber. The hospital expanded as did the office in town: electricity had replaced coal oil lamps. But while the Duncan holdings grew, they did so without its patriarch and matriarch. Death hadn't touched the family until 1913. Flynn had a little too much scotch at the annual Thanksgiving celebration, tripped on a rug, and fell down the stairs breaking his neck. He was seventy-four. He was buried with a brand new bottle of scotch whiskey; somehow that seemed fitting. Ragan finally got to see the world, but not the way he imagined. He was killed in the battle in the Ardennes August 21 to 23, WWI. He was twenty-eight. Gwenny passed on two years after Flynn at seventy-six. She just plain wore her heart out; it stopped beating October 17, 1915. Quinn lived his life full tilt; he never slowed down; he never quit. That was until a bronc got the better of him and threw him into a gate post fracturing his skull on March 15, 1918. He was eighty. Dahteste died three months later almost to the day of Quinn's passing June 16, 1918, she was seventy-eight. The death certificate said cause of death was natural causes, but those who knew her and Quinn say she died of a broken heart. They were buried together on the rise they rode to most evenings overlooking Hay's Creek.

The Duncans left a legacy unmatched in the history of the Southwest. Perhaps there were those more famous: John Chisholm, Charles Goodnight, Oliver Loving, and others. But the DD Ranch was the first to combine Apaches, Mexican vaqueros, and white buckaroos that spans five generations.

Epilogue

In the distance, two riders could be seen climbing the rise to the old Double D main gate. A man and a woman loped along easily in the warm autumn afternoon. Obviously both were experienced riders used to long days working cattle. But the woman was unfamiliar with the territory.

"Dang! is all this country one ranch?" the young woman asked.

"Yeah, pretty much," her companion explained. "While the ranch was divided up into sections that belonged to each of the Duncan heirs, the whole five hundred thousand acres are the DD Ranch holdings. The whole thing is deeded land: no lease, no BLM land."

"Wow, half a million acres. That's hard to wrap your head around," the woman said.

"Up ahead here is what I wanted to show you."

The ranch foreman led the woman up the grown over road to an old crumbling house.

"This is the original homestead where Flynn and Gwenny lived."

The two dismounted to explore the buildings more closely.

"Over there is Quinn and Dahteste's house, or at least what's left of the place. There was a fire in the forties and there was no one so inclined to rebuild. Everyone figured there wasn't anyone cut in the same cloth as Quinn and Dahteste to take over the residence. You know, folks figured there were too many ghosts . . ."

"Yeah, I understand that. You can feel the spirits in this land."

The young woman walked over to a large live oak.

"So this is the famous parlay tree?"

"Yes, ma'am." The cowboy laughed. "There was a whole lotta scotch consumed under this tree."

"So I've been told . . ."

"C'mon, we'll ride up to Hay's Creek where the graves are."

The two remounted and galloped the short way to the bluff overlooking the creek.

"OMG!" the young woman gasped. "What a breathtaking view!"

"You bet; nowhere else like this. Quinn and Dahteste used to ride up here every evening, weather permitting. They'd talk, but mostly they just sat quietly enjoying each other's company."

"The graves are well kept, not abandoned . . ."

"Yeah, you can bet there'd be hell to pay if this place was neglected. In fact, some members of the family wanted to build a big ol' monument. But these two weren't about monuments made of stone; they wanted their descendants to be living monuments."

"Simple wooden crosses. I'd say that is appropriate. 'Here lies Quinn Duncan and his beloved wife Dahteste: Born Feb 12, 1838, Died March 15, 1918. Dahteste Duncan, born 1840, died June 16, 1918.'"

The young woman traced the weathered letters reverently.

"Yes, sir, JD, these are your great, great grandparents. Along with your great, great uncle Flynn, these are the folks that started the Double D," Jeff explained.

"They lived to see my dad bein' born then, huh, Jeff," JD observed. "My father was born in 1917."

"That's right," Jeff replied. "Your grandfather was born on October 20, 1890. Did you know him?"

"You bet!" JD laughed. "He was a tough old bird. He lived to be eighty-five; he died in 1975. My dad passed in 2005 . . .

eighty-eight; they all lived to be fairly old . . . there must be some good genes flowing through the Duncan veins."

"If ya don't mind me asking, how is it ya never came down here to your family?" Jeff asked.

"I don't know. There isn't a very good answer," JD admitted. "You know how things go . . . ya get busy with your own place and problems and ya kinda forget about everybody else. Other than the few trips Dad and I made down here when I was a kid, well . . . but I'm here now and I promise you, this ranch will stay in the Duncan family forever if I have anything to say about things."

"Hey you two!" a mounted buckaroo yelled. "C'mon! They're ready for you at the ranch headquarters."

Jeff and JD mounted up and galloped to join the other hand and together the rode the three miles to the new ranch headquarters. Another hand took their horses and together Jeff and JD walked up the steps of the ranch house.

"Whooie," JD breathed. "This place bespeaks of a whole lotta money."

"Ain't that the truth," Jeff replied.

They walked into the library and were greeted by several men dressed in suits. New York lawyers, JD thought. Wonder what Quinn would have thought about this? Probably woulda filled their backsides with a load of rock salt and sent them on their way. Too bad, there is a lot to be said about frontier justice, JD sighed. Tyler Hanson, the Duncan family attorney introduced JD to all the suits. Let's try to be polite . . . for now . . . JD reasoned.

Harmon Castleford was what was known as a shark in the business world. He ran hostile takeovers for predatory corporations. He was very good at his job. He had never lost until he ran up against JD Duncan. When he saw her enter the study, cold chills ran up and down his spine.

"Well, we meet again." Castleford smiled.

JD always said she felt like she needed to take a hot shower after a meeting with this sleaze bag.

"Seems like it," JD replied curtly, ignoring the man's proffered handshake. "Now let's get this done."

"Of course," the sleazy lawyer said. "The papers are all in order, JD . . ."

"I didn't realize we were on a first name basis," JD growled.

"Yes, of course, Ms. Duncan. Well, all we need to turn the Duncan holdings over to the consortium is your signature here."

He directed her attention to the line at the bottom of the document. JD took the papers from the attorney.

"Really, the papers are all in order, a signature is all that's required."

"You don't say," JD responded. "Well, I never sign anything unless I read the whole thing." She emphasized the word "whole."

For the next hour, JD read the entire ten page contract. When she finished, she laid the contract on the table and stood up. She admired the antique gun collection on the wall behind the desk. She took a shotgun off the wall, cracked open the barrel to see if there were any shells in the chamber . . . there were. She closed the barrel and set the gun on the desk as she sat back down. She spun the contract around and around on the shiny mahogany desk, then fingered the shotgun with her other hand. She addressed her next comment to Jeff.

"Ya know, Jeff, ya ought not to leave these things loaded; someone might get hurt."

"Yes, ma'am," the foreman replied. "You are dead-bang right about that."

JD nodded, then turned back toward the New York lawyer.

"Castleford, you know me, you know what I am capable of doing. My daddy didn't raise a fool. So, you see, I know a swindle when I see one. There isn't going to be a transfer of one inch of the Double D. You might just as well have tried to catch the wind . . . you'd have been just as successful. And if you try going after the Jicarilla, I will tie you up in so many legal knots, you will never get free . . . then, I'll sue you for every penny you and your so called consortium has. I hope I've made myself clear."

Castleford and his crew were struck dumb. They were sure this was a done deal. Obviously, they were wrong. But they were nothing if they weren't persistent.

"You don't have enough members of the family to back you and if you think you can call those Indians family . . ."

JD cut him off in mid-word. "Oh you are so wrong. I can count the Jicarilla as family . . . you are talking to a Jicarilla or had you forgotten who my great, great grandmother, my grandfather and grandmother were. Now, I may not be full blood Apache, but if you have one drop of Native blood, you are Native. We're done here."

JD raised the shotgun until it was pointing at the ceiling and she fired off one barrel. Everyone in the room, except JD, jumped a little. The suits from New York nearly wet themselves.

"See Jeff." JD smiled. "See how easy these darn things can go off? They're damn dangerous." She turned to the housekeeper, Beth. "Beth, would you please see to it the ceiling gets fixed."

"Yes, ma'am," she replied.

"Oh and you can send these gentlemen the bill. Jeff would you please show these folks out and have some of the boys escort them off the property. Thank you."

Now that was kinda fun, JD thought, uhuh, uhuh, uhuh. But she knew this was only the opening salvo in this legal battle, but she was assured in her ability to win any fight . . . that was built into her genetic makeup. JD scanned the room until her eyes lit on a portrait of Quinn and Dahteste. Painted after the couple had reached their seventies, age had not lessened the sharp, intense countenance of the pair. They were still people to be reckoned with. JD smiled and spoke to her great grandparents.

"As long as I'm alive, no one will ever destroy this land or take the land away from your people, grandmother."

How 'bout that? JD chuckled to herself; me, Jennifer Dylan Duncan, the caretaker of the Duncan family legacy. Who'da thunk it . . .

T.K. Galarneau was born and raised in North Central Idaho in a small farming and ranching community called Nezperce where she graduated in 1969. She received a BS degree in English and History from Lewis-Clark State College in Lewiston in 1973. Terrie taught English and Reading in the Lewiston school district until moving to California in 2001 to continue her teaching career. She now makes her home in the Bay Area with two dogs, three cats, and two horses. When she's not teaching or writing, she spends most of her time riding.

Visit her website: http://bunkhouseramblin.weebly.com

Just aim your phone camera at the QR Code